# SLAY BELLS RING

## A CHRISTMAS COZY MYSTERY: BOOK TWO

### MONA MARPLE

New Year's Eve in Candy Cane Hollow.

I had to pinch myself as I stretched and sat up in bed. The view from my window was just as if someone had taken a white blanket and covered the ground with it.

Another fresh snowfall had come down overnight. I'd never seen snow like it!

There was a soft rap on the door and before I could answer, in walked Mrs Claus. She was wearing a red velour tracksuit with the Claus Crest emblazoned on the chest pocket.

"Wow, look at you," I said as I wiped the sleep out of my eyes.

"Sorry to disturb you dear, but you did say you wanted to join me this morning," Mrs Claus said.

"I sure did," I agreed. As soon as Mrs Claus had told me about her tradition of visiting all of the local businesses on New Year's Eve, I'd decided it would be a great way to see more of Candy Cane Hollow.

"I'm making porridge. We don't want you setting out on an empty stomach," Mrs Claus said.

"You're having some too?" I asked.

Mrs Claus giggled. "The rest of us have already had breakfast. Come on down when you're ready, dear."

She left the room and pulled the door closed behind her. I reached for my phone and tapped it to see the time - almost 11am!

I groaned. I couldn't remember the last time I'd slept in so long, never mind while I was a guest in someone else's home!

I darted up and had a quick shower, dried my hair and pulled on a jumper dress, tights and knee boots.

A round of applause broke out as I entered the kitchen, and at least I had the decency to blush a little.

"I'm so sorry," I began.

"Nonsense, you clearly needed your rest," Father Christmas himself said. He leaned back in his chair, his hands clasped across his big belly, a twinkle in his eyes. That twinkle had never left his eyes since I'd first met him, and I was starting to think it was a permanent feature.

"I for one am grateful that you slept in for most of the day. It gave Mrs Claus a chance to reveal how she truly feels about my cooking," Gilbert, the elf, exclaimed.

"What are you talking about?" Mrs Claus asked with a laugh.

"I prepared your breakfast and now you're insisting that you make the porridge for Holly. Perhaps I should hang up my apron and become a reindeer trainer!"

"Oh, Gilbert," Mrs Claus said as she continued to stir the porridge. It smelt amazing but I didn't dare say that.

"A reindeer trainer? I can't see that! You've been

pampered indoors for too long, Gilbert," Father Christmas said with a belly laugh.

"I know people. I could find a job on the reindeer circuit. What's that person called? Lilly-Rue? Peggy-Sue? Annie-Poo?"

"Annie-Poo?" Nick asked as he joined us in the kitchen. I swallowed as I saw him, and as our eyes met a jolt of electricity passed between us.

"Something like that. She's a distant relative. Anyway, since my cooking skills aren't up to much, I'll go and polish the baubles," Gilbert shrugged.

"Thank you, dear," Mrs Claus called, but he had already left.

"He really is quite dramatic, isn't he?" I asked.

"He's a very, erm, spirited elf," Mrs Claus said with a wink.

"That's one way of putting it," Nick smiled and revealed the dimple in his cheek. I looked away but not before I felt my cheeks flame.

"Holly's joining me this morning on my little visit to the local businesses. Isn't that lovely, Nick?"

"Yes, mum. It'll be a great chance for Holly to explore Candy Cane Hollow more."

"And what are you doing today?" I asked him.

"Dad and I are going over the stats from Christmas, seeing how the delivery run went."

"Don't tell me even Santa has targets!" I joked.

Nick grimaced. "It's all about the APDS - Average Present Delivery Speed."

"Don't forget the LPT - Lost Present Tally. The elves can really get grumpy if they feel a present they worked on got lost in transit!" Father Christmas added.

"Which I can understand. They work hard," Nick said.

"That's enough work talk. Nick, you need to improve your conversation skills. Why don't you ask Holly more interesting questions, like what she sees in a man or where her ideal first date would be?" Mrs Claus asked.

"Mother!" Nick exclaimed.

I giggled, and ate my porridge.

Ever since Mrs Claus had rescued me from a snowy car crash and brought me to Candy Cane Hollow, I'd been trying to fight my attraction to Nick. And failing.

"I'm ready," I said. I pushed my chair back and picked up my bowl, just as Gilbert returned to the room.

"Let me guess. You're washing your own dishes now, too? I'll be jobless and homeless for the New Year at this rate!"

"Oh, Gilbert, don't be silly," Mrs Claus soothed.

I placed my bowl back on the table, as much as it pained me not to use my manners and tidy away after myself.

"I was just going to rinse it so the porridge didn't dry, but..."

"Holly Wood! You imagine this to be a residence where porridge is allowed to dry on a bowl? Jumping Jack Frost, if my mother could see what I've become. I'll wash that bowl right away and then get my coat!"

Nick stifled a laugh and I followed Mrs Claus into the hallway and put on my coat, gloves and scarf.

"Are we taking Baby?" I asked.

"No, you're not!" Father Christmas's booming voice came from behind us.

"A sleigh will be safer in this weather, dear," Mrs Claus said and gave me a wink.

"You were going to take Baby, weren't you?" I whispered as soon as we'd said our goodbyes and left Claus Cottage.

"Of course I was! But my husband has a good point. We'll save the Cadillac for another day. Oh!"

"Oh?"

"You will be here, won't you, dear? We're all hoping so much that you'll make this more of a permanent situation."

"I'd like to," I admitted with a smile. I'd never seen anywhere as magical as Candy Cane Hollow and still felt disbelief that the place really existed.

"That's settled then. We'll just sort out the finer details. Oh, Holly, I'm so glad I found you! Now, let's go and spread some festive cheer with our hard working town folk!"

Mrs Claus was small and slight, but she controlled the sleigh as well as she did the baby pink Cadillac. The pair of reindeer who pulled us across the snowy landscape obeyed her every command and we were on the High Street before I knew it.

"First stop, The Greasy Spoon!" Mrs Claus declared as she practically jumped down from the sleigh. I got down too, although nowhere near as gracefully as she had.

In Candy Cane Hollow, the Claus family were practically royalty, and every person and elf we saw was overcome with excitement when they spotted us.

Mrs Claus knew everyone by name and gave everyone a personal greeting, asking about children and second cousins and whether the result of that medical test had come back yet. It was mighty impressive to watch.

"It's the most wonderful time of the year!" A woman with a triple pushchair called out to us.

Mrs Claus and I waved to her, even as I calculated that we must be almost 360 days away from the next Christmas.

"It's always Christmas here, isn't it?" I asked.

"We have the spirit of Christmas all year around! It's marvellous!"

"Wow. And everyone loves you, that's obvious."

"This is the work that goes along with being Mrs Claus, dear. It's the best job in the world."

"I can believe it," I said, but I knew there was a deeper meaning behind her words. Mrs Claus was desperate to see Nick settled down, and I realised that she was having me join her so I could see what could be in my future if she got her way.

Not that I was against the idea of spending a lifetime gazing into Nick Claus' eyes. And that dimple, oh my.

Mrs Claus was about to push open the door to The Greasy Spoon, a cafe that I'd never set foot in before, when someone opened the door from within.

"Mrs Claus won't be opening the door for herself on my watch, oh no Sir! Come, come, take a seat, what'll it be?" A short and immaculately dressed man asked. He was wearing a glittery red blazer and his facial hair was trimmed to perfection.

"Twisty! How kind of you. Holly and I would love some of your famous winter berry tea, if that's not too much trouble?"

"Nothing could ever be too much trouble for you, Mrs Claus!"

"Bacon sarnie for the gals too?" An older and rotund elf with a gleaming bald spot appeared from the kitchen and wiped his hands on his apron.

"Greasy! There you are!" Mrs Claus exclaimed.

"Alright, Mrs C?"

"Mrs Claus will certainly not be eating a *bacon sarnie*, Greasy. I could make a lovely smashed avocado and pancetta on sourdough, though?"

"They want their bellies full of proper food, mate, none of this fancy stuff!" Greasy rolled his eyes.

"Just the tea will be fabulous, really, we have a busy day

ahead and we ate at home. But both of your suggestions sound wonderful. Another day!" Mrs Claus said diplomatically.

Greasy humphed and returned to the kitchen.

"I'm beginning to realise that being Mrs Claus is quite the political position," I murmured.

Mrs Claus laughed and her eyes twinkled with mischief, but she was far too polite to respond.

"I'm guessing he's the owner and The Greasy Spoon is named after him?"

"Greasy and Twisty are business partners, they own the place jointly," Mrs Claus explained.

Twisty returned to our table with beautiful glassware, and poured us each a glass of amaranth coloured tea. It smelled divine.

"I was just explaining to Holly here that you and Greasy own this delightful place," Mrs Claus said.

"We sure do. We've been in business together almost two years now."

"That's a brave decision for people with different ideas about food," I said with a smile.

Twisty raised an eyebrow and gave a mock pout. "I'm trying to teach him a more refined palate but you know what they say... Rome wasn't built in a day!"

"Well, good luck, dear," Mrs Claus laughed.

A series of bangs and crashes came from the kitchen and Twisty offered his apologies.

"Twisty!" Greasy pushed open the kitchen door and glared across at his business partner.

I watched as a woman who sat alone in the far corner took out a notepad and jotted something down.

"Greasy, we have customers. Keep your voice down! Whatever's wrong?"

"Don't mind us, it sounds like a stressful morning. Is everything okay, Greasy?" Mrs Claus asked.

"Unprofessional," the woman in the corner said with a tut.

"Peggy-Sue, I'm sorry! What are you writing there? Nothing serious, I hope? Can I refill your tea?" Twisty gushed.

"Did you hide the ketchup?" Greasy stomped across the cafe and squared up to Twisty, who flinched and took a step back.

"No!"

"You liar! You've taken the ketchup! How dare you come into my kitchen and mess with..."

"Your kitchen?" Twisty exclaimed.

"It's my name on the door, pal!"

"And wasn't that a mistake? I just thought it was a funny play on words, but it's gone right to your big, shining, bald head!"

Mrs Claus gasped. "Now, Twisty..."

"I'm sorry, Mrs Claus, I don't know what came over me!" Twisty said. His eyes filled with tears.

Greasy tore off his apron and stomped towards the door.

"Where are you going, dear?" Mrs Claus called after him.

"To buy more ketchup, of course! And I'll be keeping it locked away out of *his* reach!"

With that, Greasy stormed out of The Greasy Spoon and trudged away in the snow.

"Oh, dear," Mrs Claus said.

"Unprofessional! Incredibly unprofessional! To walk out during opening hours, in front of you of all people, Mrs Claus. I can't get my head around such behaviour!"

"But, Twisty, why did you take the ketchup?"

Twisty froze, open-mouthed. "I..."

"Don't lie, dear. I've known you since you were in a pushchair. Whatever were you thinking?"

Twisty placed his hands on his cheeks and let out a sigh. "That elf has an unnatural love for ketchup, Mrs Claus. I've never seen anything like it. He'll add it to anything! How are we ever going to become a more upmarket place if he's classing ketchup as a main food group?"

I stifled a laugh.

"I know it's frustrating, dear."

"Here's an idea. Why don't you introduce a condiment station out here. Then the customers can add ketchup if they want to. You can put out some nice dips and garnishes as well, things you'd like to see people try more often," I suggested.

Twisty considered the idea then burst into a grin. "I love it! I'll get on to that right away, before You Know Who can object to the idea! I can sure see why Santa has you on his nice list."

I felt my cheeks flame and gave an awkward laugh.

Mrs Claus said nothing, but gave me a warm smile and a slight nod. We drank our tea and then it was time to move on and pay another Candy Cane Hollow business a festive visit.

## 2

M rs Claus and I finished our visits right in time to return to Claus Cottage for lunch.

None of the other visits had been as eventful as the first. We'd visited The Polar Arms, where Ginger Rumples had pulled a pint for each of us despite the early hour, and Sleigh A While, a fairly new and upmarket coffee shop.

We'd admired the latest collection of clothes in Winter Warmers, and Mrs Claus had shown me her favourite kitchen accessories in Ho-Ho-Home from Home.

Every shop owner had been excited to see us and their warmth was infectious. I realised just how special Mrs Claus was and what an excellent job she did of making everyone in town feel valued.

We even went across town to Candy Cane Custody, where Chief Superintendent Wiggles made us hot choco-lates and shared his concerns about the latest crime spree in the town - a chestnut tree had been stripped bare overnight, which went against the town's *Only Take Your Fair Share* rule.

Back at Claus Cottage, Gilbert had managed not to walk

out and was instead checking on jacket potatoes as if his life depended on it.

"The skin must be crispy! And I can't open the oven and check, that would ruin it," he said. He was cross-legged on the kitchen floor, gazing in through the oven's glass panel.

"Oh, Gilbert, the lengths you go to for us. Thank you, dear!" Mrs Claus exclaimed. She clearly thought that the sensitive elf was in need of a compliment.

"Where are the others?" I tried to sound nonchalant.

"Your Santa in shining armour is still at work. Father Christmas too. There's no rest for the wicked! Their jacket potatoes will be ruined, because of course nobody tells Gilbert when they'll be home," the elf muttered to himself.

"That's a good point. I'll be sure to mention it to them," Mrs Claus said as we left the kitchen.

In the den, Mrs Claus flicked on the TV. It was constantly switched to the Christmas movies channel and they played out in the background.

"So, what did you think of our little tour today?" Mrs Claus asked.

"I had a really great time. I found it fascinating getting to see the local businesses and meet more people - and elves."

"We have such a wonderful community here, Holly. And we really do welcome new people," Mrs Claus said. She was many things but subtle wasn't one of them.

"I do want to stay. I guess it's all just happening so fast. I didn't even know this place existed a few days ago!"

Mrs Claus shook her head. "Oh, listen to me. I don't want to put you under any pressure. I have some thank you cards to write out so I'll leave you to it for a while, is that okay?"

"Sure," I said. I'd never met anyone who wrote as many

thank you cards as Mrs Claus. It was a wonder that she hadn't developed RSI.

Mrs Claus went off to her study and I watched the Christmas movie for a few minutes, enjoying the peace and quiet.

And then my phone rang.

"August!" I exclaimed as I answered.

"Hey there, big sis. Happy New Year!"

"Happy New Year's Eve! Do you guys have plans?" I asked. My sister had her life all sorted. She lived in a beautiful cottage with her handsome husband Tom and adorable baby, Jeb.

"We're having a quiet one at home. I have a dozen or so friends coming over and I'm making a roast beef dinner with all the trimmings. We have some champers chilling ready for the big countdown because, well, it is NYE! Are you sure you don't want to come across and join us? We'd love to see you."

"I actually have plans," I admitted.

"You dark horse! Tell me everything!"

"Well, I met this guy," I said. I could feel myself blushing as I spoke.

"Shut the front door! Are you kidding me right now? Why am I only just hearing about this?"

"Well, you guys just had Jeb's first Christmas. I didn't want to bore you..."

"Enough. This could never be boring. I demand that you tell me absolutely everything right now," August said. She was definitely the bossy sister.

"His name is Nick, and he's really nice," I said. I was doing a totally lame job of putting Nick Claus into words.

"And where is he taking you tonight? Please say somewhere terribly glamorous and sophisticated so I can live through you!"

"Your own plans sound pretty glamorous and sophisticated to me. A dozen or so friends, a dinner and champagne in your lovely cottage!"

"Don't change the subject," August told me.

"He's asked me to be his date at a New Year's Eve Ball," I said.

"Oh-em-gee. Did you hear that bang? That was me just fainting with envy. A Ball? I am so excited for you, Holly! This one sounds like a keeper!"

"Steady on, I haven't known him long," I said, although everything in my body told me that Nick Claus was indeed a keeper.

"What are you wearing?"

"Oh," I said.

"You have sorted your outfit, right?"

"Yes, I just don't know how to explain it to you. It's a dress, and it's long, and it's red."

"Please tell me it shows off your shoulders? They really are one of your best features," August said.

"It does indeed show my shoulders," I said.

"You're wearing your hair up, right? Maybe a couple of tendrils tumbling down? Man, I wish I could come over and help you get ready but we have this photoshoot for Jeb and..."

"A photoshoot?" I asked.

"All of the mums are doing it, a New Year's Eve photoshoot. It's Jeb with these props that kind of sum of what this year has been about, to us as a family and to the world. It's pretty intense, we had to buy like sixteen outfit changes for him," August breathed.

"Wow. You'll have to send a photo," I said, although in

reality I preferred the occasional photo that she sent me where Jeb looked like a baby, not a professional model.

My favourite had been one she'd sent where he had yoghurt smeared across the whole of his face and even in his hair. She'd asked me to delete it an hour later, but I hadn't.

"Sure, I'll send you the link and you can choose which package to order!"

"Great!" I said.

"Ugh, I have to go. It's almost the witching hour. If Jeb naps any longer he won't be in bed on time tonight."

"You're not letting him stay up to see in his first New Year?" I asked.

"Absolutely not. The first rule of sleep training is consistency, Holly. If we make an exception for New Year's Eve, all of a sudden we'll be making them for weekends and then every night that Tom gets home from work late. It's a slippery slope."

"It sounds it," I agreed.

"I'll ring you tomorrow and I want you to tell me every last detail. Okay?" August asked, but she ended the call before I could reply.

I spread out on the sofa and then, perhaps inspired by baby Jeb, fell fast asleep.

## 3

I might have had no words to describe my dress other than long and red, but I was pleased to see that whatever the style was, it suited me.

August was right, my shoulders were a good feature of mine. I'd been a little insulted by that for many years, the fact that while other women seemed to have amazing hair or beautiful faces, my bodily strength was an area that was usually covered and hardly seemed deserving of any headlines.

And yet, the dress I'd selected for the Ball was beautiful. It clung in the right places and then didn't cling in the, erm, other places.

I gave my reflection a nod of satisfaction and opened the door of the bedroom I was staying in.

I squealed as I almost ran straight in to Gilbert.

"What the heck? You scared me!" I exclaimed.

The elf gave me a cheeky grin and then pulled a funny face, as if hoping to scare me again.

"What are you doing creeping around?"

"Creeping? I just dragged the vacuum cleaner upstairs.

You'd have heard me coming a mile away if you hadn't been so busy talking to yourself," Gilbert said with a giggle.

"I was not talking to myself."

"Oh, yes you were," he insisted.

"Saying what?" I crossed my arms and looked at him with a challenge on my face.

"*Oh, Holly, you got it going on girl!*"

"You're kidding me?" I asked.

Gilbert snickered and walked past me, the vacuum cleaner clunking along after him.

I was sure I'd said no such thing. But I decided not to continue the conversation. Even if I had said something like that, it was only to boost my confidence. It had been a long time since I'd had a date with a gorgeous, dimpled man.

I walked downstairs carefully, wary of the length of my dress, and found Mrs Claus waiting for me in the hall.

"Oh, Holly," she breathed as she saw me.

"Are you crying?" I asked with concern.

"I certainly am, dear. You're a vision in red. How beautiful and festive you look!"

"Really? Thank you!"

Mrs Claus looked incredible herself, in a deep red dress and a white fur shrug around her shoulders.

We grabbed our shoes and headed out to an ornate sleigh, complete with chauffeur waiting.

"Now, you know I can handle this thing myself, dear," Mrs Claus addressed the man as he held his hand out to help her climb in.

"I don't doubt it for a moment, but I'm under strict orders to look after you the way you look after everyone else," the man said with a chuckle.

He offered me his hand and I allowed him to help me up

into the sleigh. He draped a thick blanket across our laps and then we were off, dashing through the snow.

We arrived at the venue within minutes and as soon as Mrs Claus and I entered, all eyes were on us. That was the Mrs Claus magic, it happened everywhere she went and I felt lucky to be by her side.

Tables were spread around the outside of a large dance floor, and an enormous glitter ball rotated from the ceiling.

"You like?" Nick appeared by my side and handed me a glass of Champagne.

"It's surreal, being here with you and your family. This place looks incredible," I gushed. I didn't say that Nick looked incredible, even though the thought had entered my head. He was wearing a tuxedo and he looked like a chiseled, dark-haired 007.

"Lila! You've outdone yourself, dear!" Mrs Claus addressed a small woman who looked incredibly serious.

"That's very kind, thank you. I really must go and check on the sound, though. Excuse me," the woman gave us each a quick smile, then moved off into the crowd.

"Lila's in charge of organising the Ball. She does an excellent job every year," Mrs Claus explained.

"No wonder she looked a little stressed. There must be a lot of work involved in an event like this," I said.

"Oh, yes, I'm sure there is!" Mrs Claus agreed.

The song changed and Nick raised his eyebrows at me.

"What?" I asked with a laugh.

"May I have this dance?"

I gave him a shy nod and allowed him to lead me out onto the dance floor. We were the first people on there and a whoop erupted from the crowd, who gathered around to watch. I was aware of the flash of several cameras going off as we moved in sync.

Yes, Nick Claus could dance. Of course he could. I was beginning to wonder if there was anything the man couldn't do.

Being so close to Nick made it hard for me to concentrate on anything else, but he led me through the dance as if it was the most natural thing in the world. When I got carried away thinking about the scent of his aftershave, he realised I was about to stumble before I did and turned it into a choreographed dip.

As he pulled me upright again, I met Mrs Claus' gaze and cringed as she gave a thumbs up.

"Is this the best first date you've ever had?" Nick asked.

I frowned. The confidence wasn't like him and I wasn't sure what to make of it.

"You literally have my mother over there watching and applauding. It's smooth, right? The kind of first date that beautiful women like you dream of?"

I laughed, relieved that he was being modest rather than ultra-confident.

"Beautiful... hold on, did you call me beautiful?" I asked.

"I did," he gazed right into my eyes as he spoke and I felt my heart race.

"I don't know how to deal with compliments," I admitted.

"Just say thank you. Or you can kiss me, if you prefer," he winked.

I leaned in and planted a kiss on his lips, and heard the crowd give a collective gasp. I was sure I caught a glimpse of Mrs Claus punching the air in celebration.

I pushed all of that out of my mind and allowed myself to sink in closer as a slow song came on next. Other couples joined us on the dance floor and I lost myself in the music, in the rhythm, in the movement of my body linked with Nick's.

"Shall we get a drink?" I suggested after a few more tracks. My shoes weren't completely practical and my feet were beginning to ache.

"Sure thing," Nick agreed. We returned to the Claus table, where Father Christmas shot Mrs Claus a warning glance.

"What?" She exclaimed.

"Don't say a word," Father Christmas said with a smile.

"What are you worried I'd say, dear? I think they make a wonderful couple. The only things I want to say are nice and positive. We do have to make Holly feel welcome in our family."

"Based on a few dances and a kiss? Let them be young and have fun without asking them for a wedding date," Father Christmas commanded.

Mrs Claus quickly turned her head to me. "Did he say wedding date?"

I laughed. "You'll be the first to know!"

"Well, dear, Nick should be the first to know really. I'll be happy if I'm second."

"Very reasonable," Father Christmas muttered.

Nick returned to the table with drinks for everyone, and took the seat next to me.

The music stopped and a snazzy dressed man took to the stage.

"Good evening, ladies and gentlemen. I'm Michael Bauble and I'm here to entertain you fine folks for the next few hours. Now would be an excellent time to top up your drinks while my band and I get set up."

Nick reached for my hand. I allowed him to intertwine his fingers with mine.

The dance floor cleared as everyone followed Michael Bauble's suggestion and joined the lines for the bar.

Just a couple of stragglers remained on the dance floor, and I realised that one of them was the chef from The Greasy Spoon. He staggered across the dance floor, clearly already drunk, although he looked pretty dapper in a suit and a pair of gold loafers.

"Oh dear," I murmured.

"There's always someone who goes crazy at the start of the night. Typically, they spend the evening curled up asleep in a corner of the room," Nick said with a grin.

"Sounds like every office party I've ever been to," I said.

"And have you ever been the drunk by 8pm kind of person?" Nick asked.

"I'm afraid I've always been too sensible for that. Too worried about what other people might think. As a doctor, I've always felt a bit nervous that any escapades could get out and damage the reputation of the profession."

"I understand that feeling," Nick confided.

"Being Santa must feel like a huge responsibility," I said.

"Not just that, but following in my dad's footsteps? I mean, that guy is Christmas personified."

"And you will be, too. You'll be an excellent Santa, in your own way."

Nick looked at me and smiled, and that delicious dimple smiled at me too.

There was a creak, a groan, and then what sounded like an explosion. Someone screamed, and before I knew what was happening, Nick was shoving me down to the ground and under the table.

I cowered under there and saw that Father Christmas had done the exact same thing to Mrs Claus.

"What's happened?" I whispered.

Mrs Claus placed a finger over her mouth.

I realised that although the men had pushed us to the ground, they weren't under the table with us. Whatever had happened, they were out there dealing with it.

Before I could doubt myself, I emerged from under the table and surveyed the scene.

Right in the middle of the dance floor was the enormous glitter ball. The whole thing had somehow collapsed from the ceiling.

And sticking out from underneath it were a pair of legs. A pair of legs that ended with a pair of gold loafers.

# 4

_____

"Is that Greasy?" I called as I ran across Nick's side.

"You know him?" Nick asked with a frown.

"Your mum and I went to The Greasy Spoon this morning. He's the chef there."

"What do we do?" Nick asked.

One thing I'd learned about being a medic was that you were never really off duty. All it took was any kind of medical situation and you were back at work.

But a person crushed by a falling glitter ball? That was out of my skill set.

"I don't know," I admitted. I walked around the glitter ball and saw that it had crushed Greasy's torso. His head hadn't been hit and his eyes were still open, although it was clear he wasn't alive. A stunned expression was etched onto his face.

I took a deep breath and leaned in, then took his pulse.

The first rule of medical school: never assume that a dead person is really dead. Come to think of it, that would be a good rule for a lot of films where they punch or shoot the bad guy once and the viewers all know that person isn't dead.

I looked up at Nick and gave a tiny shake of my head.

Greasy had squirted his last ketchup.

"Is he... oh my... Greasy?" Twisty was by my side, with his mouth covered.

"If you're going to be sick, can you move away first?" I asked. The last thing anyone needed was vomit compromising the scene.

"I've called for an ambulance," Father Christmas announced.

I nodded. "Good. It needs to be declared officially."

"Declared? Are you saying he's dead? A goner? He's croaked?" Twisty asked. His face had turned a distinctly worrying shade of green and I ushered him away from the gruesome glitter ball scene.

"I know this is an awful tragedy. I'm so sorry," I said.

"Are you kidding? Greasy got crushed by a glitter ball and I missed the whole thing. I was in the toilet, you see, popped to the little boys' room, and I had no idea about anything."

"It's a terrible accident. I know that you and Greasy didn't always see eye to eye but this is..."

"Eye to eye? We got on like presents in a stocking!"

I frowned. "Well, this morning there was the whole ketchup thing. It just seemed like you had pretty different opinions."

"Nonsense. Greasy was a fine cook and a darn good businessman. We had differences of opinion but nothing that constituted a fall out," Twisty said with a sniffle.

"Of course," I agreed. Some people just couldn't speak ill of the dead. If Twisty wanted to remember his relationship with Greasy through rose tinted glasses, that was no business of mine.

"Now, if you're mixing me up with anyone, it's Drayton. In fact, just yesterday, he had a terrible argument with Greasy. Right in the middle of the High Street too! Bad for business, if you ask me."

"Drayton?" I asked. The name rang a jingle bell but I couldn't quite place it.

"So-called proprietor of Sleigh A While. You'd know him if you'd come across him. He has quite the eye for the ladies, and a lot of ladies have an eye for him for some reason."

"Sleigh A While, that's another cafe, right?"

"A bistro, he calls it, which is laughable. You can't just call yourself a bistro because you've turned the lighting down low. You know why most eateries turn the lights down?"

"Erm..."

"It's not for the atmosphere, let me tell you! It's to hide how bad the food looks. Plus, deprived of your sense of sight, your taste is impaired too. So you can't see how bad it looks and then you can't really taste it properly, either."

"Is that right?" I asked. I had no idea how we had strayed onto a critique of Twisty's business rival while his business partner lay dead on the dance floor.

"One hundred percent."

The crowd hushed as the paramedics raced in. I made my apologies to Twisty and returned to the glitter ball.

"Never mind crying, this is a case of Dying at the Discotheque," the female paramedic muttered to her male counterpart, who spotted me and grimaced.

"Sorry miss, gallows humour. It's the only way to get through a shift sometimes. Not to mention, this one gets a little grumpy when she has to miss a night out for work," he explained.

"I'm a GP, I get it," I said with a smile.

"Ah, alrighty then. Have you checked for a pulse?"

I nodded and crossed my arms. I suddenly felt cold and wished for sleeves.

"Obviously dead as a dodo but let's get on with the show," the female paramedic said as she bent down and repeated the steps I had taken a few minutes before.

"What a way to go. Hopefully he never saw it coming. Strange, though. These events are impeccable. Very odd that an accident like this would happen," the man said.

"He's just as dead as he was when you checked. We'll have to call for the police to move this thing off him. Where's Wiggles? He loves to strut his stuff at the New Year's Eve Ball."

I looked around the room and saw that Chief Superintendent Wiggles had lead a group of the waiting staff in efforts to cordon off the whole of the dance floor, probably in fears that something else might tumble from the ceiling.

I gave him a little wave and the senior police officer waddled across to me with a sombre look on his face.

"Sorry you had to see this, Holly," he said.

"Oh, don't worry about me. It's Greasy, from The Greasy Spoon," I explained.

"We've called it in. He's dead as a..." the female paramedic began.

Wiggles lifted a crazed eyebrow and she stopped mid sentence.

"Dead as a dead person, sir."

Wiggles shook his head morosely. "This is a loss indeed. He was a man who knew how to use a bottle of ketchup. I fear that Twisty will turn The Greasy Spoon into the kind of place that serves kale."

"Snowman forbid, sir!"

"Alright, well, I've called for back up so we can get this glitter ball moved right away," Wiggles said.

"Are you going to check the scene first?" I asked.

Wiggles cocked his head and frowned a little. "Check it for what?"

"Well, it's just... are we sure it's natural causes?"

"Definitely unnatural causes. Nothing natural at all about a giant glittering globe falling on someone. It's a tragic act of nature, is what it is."

"A freak accident," the male paramedic offered.

"That's it. The acts of nature are the weather things, aren't they? Like a snowdrift or a tornado."

"But you don't think it's worth just sweeping the scene for prints or at least taking some photographs? Once we move things, we can't ever come back and check the scene again," I said.

Wiggles gave a laugh and batted at me with his paw of a hand. "I'm not sending one of the boys out to get the fingerprint kit. We need to get this moved so we can crack on with the party. Midnight draws near and all that."

I nodded. I'd already had some experience with Wiggles and I knew that one of his main priorities was making sure that Candy Cane Hollow ticked along like clockwork.

I pulled my phone out of my clutch bag and looked across at him. "Do you mind?"

"Knock yourself out," he said with a wink, then left the dance floor.

I snapped a few photos of the glitter ball from different angles and even allowed Greasy to appear on some. Then I looked up above and took some photos of the ceilings.

There was an intricate pattern of beams up there and I guessed that the glitter ball had been secured to one, although perhaps not well enough.

Satisfied that I'd done all I could do, I forced myself to make eye contact with Greasy one last time, gave a resolute nod, and left the dance floor.

ﬔlthough the New Year's Eve Ball did continue after Greasy was covered and removed from the scene, nobody seemed to be in a celebratory mood.

Nobody left early, though. Everyone stuck it out until midnight, at which time a halfhearted cheer rang out and everyone hugged each other. More than a few people had tears in their eyes; if not for the loss of Greasy in particular, then because they'd witnessed someone meet their maker.

I hugged anyone and everyone, my voice repeating Happy New Year until the words seemed to blend together and stop making any sense.

"Are you ready to investigate another murder?" Ginger Rumples asked as she released me from a pretty intense hug. The red-haired woman was Nick's oldest friend and as close to him as a sister.

"Murder? Thankfully not. Just a tragic accident," I said.

"Really?" Ginger raised an eyebrow.

"I think so. You think different?"

"Let's just say I saw Greasy in a pretty heated conversation with Drayton yesterday," Ginger whispered.

"Oh, I heard about that. It's a big leap to assume that Drayton killed him based on one argument."

"Maybe. Except I happened to hear Drayton's last words to the dearly departed Greasy."

"You did? What did he say?" I asked. I liked to think that I wasn't interested in gossip, but really who was I kidding?

"Let's just say that Drayton mentioned crushing the competition," Ginger said, eyes wide.

I pulled her to one side, away from the general hubbub of the crowd, so we could speak more freely.

"Crushing the competition? He said those exact words?" I asked.

Ginger nodded. "It's no secret that Greasy and Drayton couldn't stand each other. They had totally different ideas of what a cafe should offer."

"Isn't a bit of rivalry good, though?" I asked.

"This went beyond rivalry. If The Greasy Spoon had a special event on one night, Sleigh A While would host something that same night and charge less. And did you hear about the food inspector?"

"No," I admitted.

"Someone called Food Standards about Sleigh A While. They said that instead of black truffle, what Drayton was actually shaving on to his fettuccine was a lump of coal," Ginger said with a giggle.

"That's so far-fetched it's funny. Let me guess, you think it was Greasy who made the call?"

"He admitted it. He was pretty proud of himself for that. Sleigh A While was closed down on a Friday night while Food Standards checked the whole place. Drayton was spitting mad."

"That's awful, but I don't know. Murder?"

"Well, you are Candy Cane Hollow's very own amateur

sleuth. If you're convinced it's an accident, I'm sure you're right," Ginger said.

She leaned in and gave me another hug, then left me alone with my thoughts.

I couldn't shake the feeling that Ginger might be right. It was an awfully big coincidence if Greasy had accidentally been crushed to death the day after Drayton had threatened to crush the competition.

"Here you are," Nick murmured. He looked good enough to eat and I felt my heart race the way it always did when I set eyes on him.

"I was just taking a minute," I explained.

"This sure wasn't the first date I'd planned for us. Are you okay?"

"I'm fine, and this has been a wonderful date. Anytime I'm with you, it's good. I feel awful for poor Greasy, though, and his family."

"I don't think he has a family," Nick said.

"Really?"

"Well, he has a family, of course. But I don't think he has any contact with them. He was a fairly cantankerous elf from what I saw and heard."

"He must have been lonely," I said.

Nick shrugged. "He had a girlfriend until recently. In fact, you've met her tonight. You remember Lila, the event manager?"

"Yes!" I exclaimed.

"That's her."

"Wow," I said. Lila was young, attractive and switched on. She wasn't the kind of woman I imagined Greasy to be in a relationship with.

"Yeah, she was pretty cut up about the split."

"Nick Claus, how do you know these things? You're

always saying how you can't keep up with everyone's lives as well as your mum does," I teased.

"Oh, I wouldn't have known that if you'd asked me earlier today, but Lila found me at the bar earlier and spent quite a while asking for my advice to win Greasy back."

"That's interesting," I said.

"I know! I think she got her Santa confused with Romeo. Although, I have to say that things are looking up for me romantically right now."

I smiled and leaned in to kiss him before I could lose the courage. He seemed surprised, but happy, and I allowed myself to sink into his embrace for a few moments, before a thought occurred to me.

I pulled away and gasped.

"What's wrong?" Nick asked.

"Greasy's ex-girlfriend is the event manager? She's the one in charge of the glitter ball!"

Nick frowned. "You're right. She must feel awful."

"Nick, what if this isn't an accident?"

"Oh, no, it has to be an accident."

"I'm not so sure. Ginger told me that she overheard Drayton threaten Greasy yesterday. He threatened to crush the competition."

Nick winced. "That's an unfortunate choice of words. But have you met Drayton? He's not a killer. Look, he's there."

I followed Nick's gaze and saw a tall, handsome man with tight curly hair and a lopsided grin on his face. He had an arm around a woman and was clearly flattering her while he undressed her with his eyes. The woman appeared to be loving every moment.

"He's a smooth operator," I murmured.

"I don't know about..."

"I'm going to introduce myself," I said.

Before Nick could stop me, I tottered across the room. Drayton eyed me up as I approached and I had the distinct sense that he was always ready to eye up any female who went near him.

"I'm so sorry to interrupt, I just had to come over and introduce myself. You're Drayton, aren't you? From Sleigh A While?"

Drayton managed to peel himself away from his lady friend and offered me his hand. When I offered my own, he clasped it, dipped in, and placed a slightly wet kiss on my palm.

"And you are?"

"Oh, my name's Holly. I'm new in town."

"Well, young attractive women are always welcome if you ask me. Hold on. Holly? You're not Holly Wood, are you?"

"That's me," I admitted.

"Is that your real name? There must be a story there! Parents with a sense of humour?"

I shrugged. "I'm a December baby. How did you hear about me, anyway?"

"I like to keep abreast of the women in Candy Cane Hollow," he said with a wink.

I looked him up and down. His suit was made from that shiny material, and he had a blood red handkerchief sticking out of his top pocket. I spotted a patch of dust on each of his knees and averted my gaze quickly.

Dust on his knees. Interesting.

"This is your partner?" I asked, with a smile at the lady he had practically been drooling over until I'd arrived.

I saw the woman smile with pride at the exact same moment as Drayton began to shake his head.

"Never mind, it's late. You must be ready to call it a night," I blurted out, desperate to stop Drayton speaking before he could disappoint the poor woman.

No doubt she'd realise how awful he was in her own time.

"Well, it's been a delight. I sure *wood* like to see you again," Drayton said, as if he'd been out for the night with me, not the woman by his side. I watched in horror as he reached into his pocket and pulled out a business card.

I accepted the card from him and then looked at the woman he was with. "Do you have a card? I'd love to find a time to chat to you more."

"Oh! I don't have a card, but you can get my details from Drayton. That sounds great," she beamed.

I said goodnight and returned to Nick, who had retrieved our coats and looked ready to call it a night.

"Did you find any clues, Poirot?" He teased.

"Well, other than learning that Drayton is clearly a ladies' man, he also had dust all over the knees of his trousers."

"What does that mean?" Nick asked.

"Well, if someone cut down that glitter ball, they had to be up in the ceiling beams. I'm guessing it's pretty dusty up there."

"You have a point."

## 6

I woke up bright and early the next day, to a fresh snowfall and the smell of bacon.

"Good morning, Miss Holly. Did you enjoy the Ball?" Gilbert asked as I joined him in the kitchen.

"I sure did, although I'm guessing you heard about what happened?"

Gilbert took his eyes off the frying pan and looked at me. "I didn't hear anything. What happened?"

"The big glitter ball fell and crushed someone to death. Greasy from The Greasy Spoon."

Gilbert gave a laugh. "Is this a joke?"

"Sadly not. He died right away but still, what a way to go. I can't believe you didn't hear about it."

"I was asleep before 9pm. I have this New Year's Day ritual. I get up before sunrise and set my intentions for the year, do a little meditation. Then I make myself a hearty breakfast to set me up right for the year. There's enough to share, though, if you want."

"That's really kind, but I'm actually heading out myself," I said. I really had planned to get up and out straight away, and something about Gilbert's demeanour told me he would prefer to finish his New Year's Day ritual alone.

"You'll be back for the luncheon?"

"The luncheon?"

"We have one every year on January 1st. It's pretty much an open house and everyone's welcome. You'll be expected to be here, as part of the Claus family."

"I'm not part of the Claus family," I reminded Gilbert.

He let out a snicker. "Not yet, officially. Trust me, you need to be here. We start at 1pm."

"Then I'll be back before then," I agreed.

I decided to walk into town because the scenery was so amazing and I didn't have a car of my own. I'd ended up in Candy Cane Hollow after my car had skidded into a snow-bank and Mrs Claus had rescued me. I still hadn't managed to track down where exactly my old rust bucket of a car had been taken to, and I had no idea how to get a sleigh ready.

The walk was enjoyable. The town centre was just a few minutes away and it was so early that the roads were empty. Everywhere was covered with a thick blanket of white snow, and the only sounds were the occasional grunts from reindeer in the fields I passed.

I quickly found Sleigh A While and a little bell jingled to signal my arrival.

A young and very pretty waitress in a uniform of black trousers, fitted white shirt and black apron greeted me and told me to choose any table.

I picked one in the window and realised that The Greasy Spoon was across the road and a few doors down the street. It was dark and there appeared to be no signs of life in there.

The waitress returned with a menu.

"Do you know what you'd like to drink? Our hot choco-late is to die for," she said. Her name tag told me her name.

"Summer? That name has to be a hoot in Candy Cane Hollow," I said with a smile.

"Right? Although I believe you're Holly Wood, so you can probably guess exactly how fun it is," the woman said.

"Touche. I'll get a coffee and the avocado smash," I said and handed the menu back to her.

"Great choice," Summer congratulated me.

"I noticed that The Greasy Spoon's not open yet. This place must do well if they open later. You get the early trade?"

"Oh, no, it's normally open much earlier. They cater to a lot of the elves on their way to Tinkertown. We don't really want that clientele."

"Oh, I see."

"They're closed now because of the glitter ball incident last night, I'd guess. I don't know if Twisty will manage on his own," Summer confided. She had pinged my order through to the kitchen on a device she held in her hand.

"It's a real shame. Do you all get on?"

"I get on with everyone. As far as I'm concerned, life's too short for these silly fall outs. And I know if I lose this job, The Greasy Spoon would be the most natural place for me to apply. So I'm not getting involved in any beef."

"Beef?" I asked.

"You know, trouble."

"Trouble about beef?"

"No, silly! Beef means trouble. I can't imagine anyone managing to have beef about beef. That would be weird. Although, you just never know with some people I guess," Summer said.

"What kind of trouble has there been?" I leaned in and hoped that Summer enjoyed gossip as much as most people did.

"Drayton - he's my boss - he thinks that The Greasy Spoon lowers the tone of the High Street. He's all about the palate, you know? Pushing boundaries and creating new taste sensations. The Greasy Spoon is more about home comforts. It's good food, I eat there. I mean, don't tell Drayton I said that."

"Your secret's safe with me. Maybe you could call it market research if he finds out," I suggested.

"Oh, girl, already done that! How do you think we have this avocado smash recipe?" Summer asked, then gave me a wink and sashayed away to greet another new customer.

I sat and looked around the place. It was dark inside, but the ambience was nice if a little stuffy. I felt pleased that I'd done my hair and put on a fairly nice outfit for the trip, whereas The Greasy Spoon had a more welcoming vibe to it.

"Ah, we meet again," Drayton's velvet voice was by my side.

I turned to him and offered a smile as he presented me with my drink.

"Hello," I said.

"To what do I owe this pleasure?"

"I was out and about and decided to give your avocado smash a try. The recipe sounds interesting," I wondered whether he would admit stealing the idea from The Greasy Spoon.

"A chef never divulges his secrets," Drayton said as he licked his lips.

"You're the chef here?"

"Goodness, no. My skills are very much of the higher level than that. I oversee everything."

"Ah," I said. In my experience, the people who liked to oversee things didn't like to actually do much.

"You've made an excellent choice. Of course, you didn't have much choice. The Greasy Spoon's not even open. This is the problem with some so-called entrepreneurs, they don't have the commitment or the professionalism. If the sign on your door says you open at a certain time, you need to be open then every day without fail."

"Greasy was killed last night," I reminded him.

"Last I knew, Twisty was in perfect health," Drayton said with a shrug.

"Physically, perhaps. But witnessing his business partner die must have been very traumatic."

"I can't comment. I wasn't there," Drayton said.

"You were there? I saw you?" I said.

"Oh, no, I arrived after all of that commotion. I had no intentions of attending an event like that. Did you know that I applied to cater the event and they chose The Greasy Spoon instead?"

"Ah. That must have been disappointing."

"It was an absolute travesty. The finest event of the year and they choose Ketchup Man as the chef? Ridiculous."

"What made you decide to go in the end?"

"The lady I was with gave me a call and asked me to be her date. She'd been let down at the last minute."

"Very gentlemanly of you to step in at short notice," I said.

He smiled and revealed his teeth. "I'm not a fan of the one-night only kind of wham-bam-thank-you escapades, but sometimes needs must. I gave her a good night and sent her off on her way this morning. Is it terrible to admit that I've already forgotten her name? Ever since I set eyes on you last night, I've been struggling to focus on anything else."

I tried to resist the urge to roll my eyes but wasn't altogether successful. "Well, that's very sweet but I'm spoken for, so please don't let me distract you too much."

"Last night's girl was spoken for too, until she wasn't. Keep hold of my card for the future, yeah?"

"I will do," I said, although I'd already thrown it away.

"Mind if I join you until your food arrives?"

"Feel free," I said. Interrogating Drayton was the reason for my early start, and if he considered the whole thing to be some kind of linguistic foreplay, that had to work to my advantage.

"Ask me anything. What would you most like to know about the man, the myth, the legend that I am?"

If he carried on that way, I wasn't sure that I'd keep any food down when it arrived. I managed to lean in and paste a smile on my face, though.

"I heard a rumour that you'd been arguing with Greasy a couple of days ago. I know it's awfully silly, but I do like gossip. I'd love to know what was said."

"Now that's a waste of a question. I thought you'd ask me where our official first date will be, or how good a kisser I am on a scale of 1 to 10. It's a 10, by the way. Hundreds of women say so."

"That's good to know. But my actual question?"

Drayton licked his lips again. "You like to keep a man on his toes, Holly. That's excellent. Okay, I'm nothing if not trustworthy, and I did say any question. There was no argument. There. I bet you wish you'd asked a better question now."

"But people heard you. People saw you."

"No, little lady. You must be mistaken. I'm an affable kind of guy."

"So you're saying that you didn't argue with Greasy, and that when Greasy was killed, you weren't even at the Ball?"

"I was at home alone. I know that will be hard for your pretty little head to believe. Handsome man like me, home alone on New Year's Eve. It makes no sense. Now, you tell me something, you say Greasy was killed. Are you thinking it wasn't an accident?"

"Oh, I don't know about that. Surely, nobody would want to murder him?"

Drayton let out a cackle and slapped his hands on the table. "Where's the queue? There would be plenty of people, trust me!"

"Really? Like who?" I asked.

"Well, Lila would have to be the obvious choice. She sets up the events, doesn't she? If you're looking for someone who could have rigged that glitter ball, she's your woman."

"That's an interesting theory," I said.

Summer reappeared at the table with my avocado smash. I couldn't quite make out the details of it because of the lighting being so low, but the smell was good.

"Summer, doll face, fetch me a tomato juice?"

Summer nodded and turned, and I watched in horror as Drayton reached across and slapped her bum. She flinched, but said nothing.

"Do your staff like you doing that?" I tried to keep my voice even as I spoke.

"The girls love it! I mean, I wouldn't be doing that to no man anyway, would I? But, yeah, these girls, they're pretty but they need the reassurance. Give them a compliment, make sure the shirt's a real tight fit, bit of a tap of the ass now and then. It's the way to a happy workplace."

"It sounds like the way to a lawsuit for sexual harassment to me," I murmured.

If Drayton heard, he chose not to respond, and when

Summer returned with his drink in a glass, he repeated the move in a stubborn way.

I ate quickly and paid, then left.

As soon as I had walked out of Sleigh A While, I dialled the number for Claus Cottage.

"Claus Cottage, Mrs Claus speaking."

"Mrs Claus, it's Holly. I've just been to Sleigh A While and I've witnessed something really troubling," I blurted out.

"Have you found the killer?"

"What?"

"I figured that must be why you're out early. You think it's foul play, don't you, dear? I do too! I wish you'd woken me. I'd love to help you investigate."

I let out a laugh and felt myself relax. Mrs Claus had that effect.

"I'd love you to help, yes please! But that's not why I'm calling. I've just been to Sleigh A While and I'm really concerned by the way Drayton behaves. I saw him slap a waitress' bum!"

Mrs Claus gasped. "Goodness gumdrops. We can't have that. I'll get Baby ready right away and drive down to have a word with him."

"Oh, Mrs Claus, should it be you? Why don't we ask Wiggles to speak to him?"

"No, dear. There's a certain level of respect that Mrs Claus commands. Some situations need a personal touch, and I think this is one of those. I'll just touch up my lipstick and I'll be there in two shakes of a snow globe."

## 7

I returned to Claus Cottage in time for the New Year's Day Luncheon. A crew of catering elves had been hired for the occasion and Gilbert was micro-managing them with ferocity.

I watched with amusement as a trail of elves carried glorious trays of meats, cheeses, chocolates and canapés into the formal dining room. Gilbert had a comment for every one of them, telling some to stand up straighter, others to smile, and then to one particular elf, "wipe your nose once more and you're on reindeer duty!"

Gilbert spotted me watching and gave me a wave.

"You look busy," I said.

"These young elves, they don't know the basics. Nobody's getting the kind of training I had!"

"You can say that again," a sour voice came from behind us. I spun around and saw Peggy-Sue, her finger extended and trailing across the top of the cabinet.

"Just what are you doing?" Gilbert asked as Peggy-Sue inspected her finger for dust.

"I refuse to eat in dirty premises. So far, so good. You cleaned especially for today?"

Gilbert puffed up his chest but his voice wavered. "Every day is cleaning day here, thank you very much."

"Ah. Well, you missed a spot in the downstairs loo, I'm afraid."

"I did no such thing," Gilbert said, but he cleared his throat and dashed away in the direction of the toilet.

"Has he really?" I asked when he was out of earshot.

Peggy-Sue sneered at me. "I haven't even been in the downstairs loo."

I widened my eyes but decided not to engage. Since I was staying in Claus Cottage for the moment, I was representing the Claus family, and it would do no good to fall out with a guest.

"Is there a vegan menu?" Peggy-Sue asked.

"Oh, I don't actually know. I haven't been part of the food prep. I'm sure we'll be able to put something together for you, though," I said. Mrs Claus wouldn't allow any guest to go hungry, I knew that much.

"And there lies the problem. The other guests receive a banquet that plenty of thought has gone into, but the lonely vegan has something put together at the last minute. It's discrimination. I may have to make my feelings known," Peggy-Sue said, and with that she stalked away, probably in search of someone else to complain to.

I made my way through the crowded house with several people greeting me and wishing me a Happy New Year. Everyone had dressed up for the luncheon and spirits were high. The excitement in the air was palpable - to be invited to Claus Cottage was a big deal for most residents in Candy Cane Hollow.

I thought again how lucky I was to have been rescued by

Mrs Claus and welcomed into her home. And the arms of her son. Anyway.

I had to find Gilbert.

He was in the downstairs toilet, as I suspected, complete with a dusting rag and a tin of beeswax.

"I think she was joking," I said.

Gilbert looked at me as if I was speaking another language. "Joking about cleaning? Why would someone do such a thing?"

"Some people have odd senses of humour."

"Peggy-Sue doesn't have a funny bone in her body. If she was lying, she did it to torment me. Lying and joking aren't the same thing, Holly."

"No, you're right," I said.

"I cannot put up with someone coming into Claus Cottage and suggesting that the highest levels of cleanliness aren't being met! I may as well just, just, just get my coat and leave!"

"I'm not sure there's any need for that. Let's give her a chance and write it off as a clumsy joke. This place looks spotless, all the time."

Gilbert gave the small room another once over, then we opened the door and walked out one after the other. That attracted a few strange glances from the new people arriving.

"Holly, there you are!" Twisty appeared and grabbed me by the arm. His face looked pale and his eyes were red, but his voice was strong and firm.

"Twisty, how are you doing?"

"I'm quite alright, although I just have to speak to you."

"Oh? Of course. What's on your mind?" I asked.

"A little angel told me that you went to Sleigh A While this morning. Is that true?"

"Erm, yes. I had breakfast there," I admitted.

"But why would you go there? With the sad loss of our dear friend, Greasy, I can assure you that The Greasy Spoon needs your support."

"It was closed," I said. I decided not to reveal that even if it had been open, I would have still gone to Sleigh A While so that I could interrogate Drayton.

"Today it was closed. It would have been insensitive to open. But we shall reopen, with a new decor and a new menu. The Greasy Spoon will be better than ever! In Greasy's memory, of course."

"I'm pleased to hear it. I'll be sure to pop in when you open again," I promised.

"Wonderful! Please, bring one of the Clauses with you. All of them, even. They really do give a place the seal of approval if they actually go there themselves."

"I'll see what I can do," I said.

"You're a star," Twisty said with a thin smile.

"You said last night you didn't actually see the accident, did you?"

"Oh, no. Little boys' room! Weak bladder. Guess I'm getting old! I came right out when I heard the commotion but thankfully, I didn't see it happen."

"That's it, the toilet. You said last night," I said. In fact, he'd given me his alibi before I'd asked for it. Was that suspicious?

"I'm glad I didn't see it. Anyway, I'll let you mingle. I know everyone wants a few minutes with you."

∽

TWISTY WAS RIGHT.

Everyone and their reindeer wanted five minutes with me.

A doddery old woman named Shirley asked me how Nick had proposed, and was mortified when I told her he hadn't actually proposed.

"But you exchanged a kiss with him at the Ball," she managed to croak with her weakened voice as she filled a plate with festive fancies.

"Ah, well spotted," I said with a wink.

"He won't be buying the cow if he's getting the milk for free. Mark my words!"

"I'll certainly remember that," I said with a grimace. I patted her arm and walked away, ignoring the rumbling of my stomach.

It wasn't worth helping myself to any food as I'd be interrupted before I could take a bite.

## 8

All I did was attempt to cover a food platter with clingfilm, and I felt Gilbert's gaze boring into me.

"That's not your job," he said. His arms were crossed and his expression was anything but jolly.

"I just thought I'd help," I said.

"Oh! I see! Gilbert is an elf who needs help to clear away after a luncheon. I get it. You think it's all too much for me? Or you've been watching the way I tidy and felt the need to do better? I should just..."

"...hang up your apron sleeves," I muttered under my breath. I was getting used to the elf's dramatics.

"...hang up my apron sleeves and retire!"

"I'm sorry, I just think it's polite to help out. You've all welcomed me into your home. I'm not used to having a household manager, remember," I decided to go with flattery rather than sarcasm.

"You're not?" Gilbert asked in disbelief.

"I live alone in London," I reminded him. Or, at least, I used to live alone in London. It was looking more and more likely that Candy Cane Hollow would be my new home.

"Ah. You're a peasant," Gilbert said with a knowing look.

"A peasant?! I'm not a peasant!" I said with a laugh.

"But you don't have house staff?"

"Nobody has house staff in London. Most people are working all day just to afford a one bedroom flat, never mind anything so luxurious as a Gilbert!"

His chest puffed up a little with that compliment. "I'll have to remember to be a little more patient with you, since you have no proper etiquette training. Try to remember that if I need your help, I'll ask you."

"Okay," I said.

"And, one more thing."

"Yes?"

"I'll never ask you."

I nodded my understanding and stood away from the table as Gilbert methodically wrapped dishes, stacked empty plates and cleared up pieces of spilled sausage roll pastry and crisps.

After a few moments, I decided to leave him to it and slip out of Claus Cottage.

I made it to the entrance hall before Mrs Claus came bounding downstairs.

"Holly! Where are you off to?"

"I was just going for a walk," I said. It was not exactly the truth, but not a lie, either.

"Fancy some company? We need to start thinking about setting you up at the surgery," Mrs Claus said.

"Do you read minds? I was literally just thinking that," I said.

Mrs Claus grinned at me with a twinkle in her eye.

We pulled on our outdoor clothes and called a goodbye to Gilbert, Nick and Father Christmas.

Snow was falling steadily and I was grateful for the gloves and hat.

"Where are you off to then, dear?"

"I just fancied a walk," I said, then immediately regretted not sharing the whole truth. Mrs Claus had made me feel so welcome.

"That's nice," Mrs Claus said.

"I wanted to go and speak to Lila. I heard she works at The Reindeer Run?"

"Oh, yes. She's one of the most skilled reindeer handlers we have. I can show you the way."

"Don't you want to know why I want to talk to her?" I asked.

"Well, I imagine it's to question her about Greasy's death. But you don't have to tell me everything, dear. I know I can be a little bit of a gossip at times. A little too into people's business. Especially people I care about."

"I know that everything points to Greasy's death being a terrible accident. I just can't shake the idea that perhaps there's more going on."

"You think the glitter ball was rigged somehow?"

"I do," I admitted. I sounded like one of those conspiracy theorists, I was sure, but Mrs Claus was too polite to laugh at me.

"Speaking to Lila makes sense then," Mrs Claus said. A pick-up truck drove slowly by and Mrs Claus automatically waved. Before I realised, I'd done the same. Candy Cane Hollow really was growing on me.

"Because of her job?"

"Her second job. The Reindeer Run is her main work. She's at the reindeer farm full-time. The event planning is more of a sideline, although she's very good at it."

"She'd be the person who set up the glitter ball?" I asked.

"I would expect so, but she does have helpers some-times. You'll have to ask her, dear."

We arrived at The Reindeer Run, which seemed to me to be some kind of 5-star hotel for reindeer. The whole thing was decked out in a simple, tasteful way, with rows of stables in different festive colours. Christmas music played out - for the staff or the animals, I wasn't sure.

The reception desk was empty, a sign propped up that declared:

*If we ain't here, we're with the 'deer!*

"Shall we wait?" I asked.

"She'll be around. Let's go and find her," Mrs Claus suggested. We left the reception area and went out to explore the stables. Most of them were empty and unbeliev-ably neat.

Behind the stables were the fields, and in the distance I could see figures moving. Several reindeer, and one person.

I watched in amazement as the reindeers responded to click commands, as if they were well-trained dogs!

One reindeer weaved in and out of some candy canes, another lay down, rolled over, then jumped into the air and did something resembling the splits. A trio of reindeer performed an identical dance routine, complete with a jazz hands finish.

The person barely moved, leading the choreographed set with a subtle head movement, a shift of a leg, and the click commands.

"Wow," I said, my breath forming a cloud as if I were a dragon breathing smoke.

"She's very talented, isn't she?"

"Its incredible," I admitted.

We continued to watch, until Lila gave a short, sharp blow of a whistle, at which point the reindeers stopped being perfectly synchronised acrobats and returned to their natural animal state. They ran and played in the snow, tussled with each other's antlers and dug around for grass to eat.

Lila began a leisurely walk across the field, appeared to stop in her tracks when she saw us, then gave a big wave and burst into a jog. She closed the gate of the field behind her so that the reindeer could continue playing safely.

"Mrs Claus! Is everything okay? I didn't know you were here, sorry," Lila said. Her cheeks were rosy red.

"That's quite alright, dear. We were passing and I realised that Holly hadn't seen your skill with the reindeer."

"You're amazing," I gushed.

"Oh, thanks. They do all of the work, though," Lila said with a shrug. She turned and gazed at the animals as she spoke. It was clear that she was mad about them.

"You must have been doing this for years," I said.

"Since I was a child," Lila agreed with a nod.

"She's like the Cesar Milan of the reindeer world," Mrs Claus said with a wink.

"Oh, I don't know about that. I say a trainer is only as good as their animals," Lila said.

"You're modest. But you do great work here, and the way you set up the Ball was amazing too."

"Oh, thanks," Lila shifted in her snow boots at the mention of the Ball.

"It was a shame it ended the way it did," I said.

"Yes, you could say that," Lila said.

"Sorry, it's insensitive of me to mention it."

"It's just... I'll never plan an event again, will I?"

"Won't you?" I asked.

"Who would want to book me after what happened? People are giving me odd looks now. I'm better here just throwing myself into my reindeers. Speaking of which, I need to get them back into their stables," Lila said.

She gave a click and I watched in amazement as the reindeers lined up by the gate in height order, smallest first. Lila unclipped the gate and lead the animals to the stables, where each reindeer entered its own stable in turn.

I looked at Mrs Claus with my eyes wide.

"Are you thinking what I am?" I asked.

"What's that, dear?"

"That there's no way someone as competent as Lila didn't fix that glitter ball to the ceiling properly."

Mrs Claus nodded. "It would certainly be a shock."

Lila closed all of the stable doors and returned her attention to us.

"I have to make up their food now, but if you want to come into the kitchen I can make us all a hot chocolate?"

"That sounds perfect," Mrs Claus accepted.

We all filed into the building through the back door, stomped our feet on the hard floor of the utility room, and we were then in the kitchen, where a roaring fire burned.

"So, you're finding that people are being different with you after the Ball?" I asked.

Lila sighed as she filled a pan with milk and switched on the hob. "I don't blame them, exactly. But I've been doing events for a long time and nobody ever died before. I get that it's suspicious."

"With Greasy being your ex?"

"Exactly. I can see people thinking that maybe I was distracted and didn't quite secure it properly."

"Do you think there's any chance that's what happened?"

Lila closed her eyes tight. "It must be what happened. No matter how good I like to think I am at my jobs, I made a mistake. A fatal mistake. And poor Greasy paid the ultimate price."

"There's no other explanation?" I pushed.

"Like what?"

"Well... Mrs Claus said sometimes you have helpers? Did anyone else go near the glitter ball?"

"Absolutely not. The helpers get to set out the tables, maybe polish the glasses although most of them aren't too great at that job. They're kids looking to earn a bit of money. I wouldn't trust them with the glitter ball."

"You can't beat yourself up too much," Mrs Claus soothed.

"Of course I can! I should! A man has died because I didn't do my job properly."

"It does look like a tough work environment, up there with the beams," I said.

"It's fine. The beams are wider than they look. There's a staircase up there and good lighting. As long as you don't mind heights, it's perfectly safe. And I've been doing the Ball for so many years, I could probably work out my way around there with my eyes closed."

Lila finished talking, and gasped.

"Listen to me. With my eyes closed! It's that attitude that caused this tragedy."

"You're being very hard on yourself, dear. Everyone makes mistakes at times."

"Do you remember fixing the glitter ball up there? Were you paying attention like you normally would?" I asked.

Lila considered the question as she stirred the milk. "I've replayed it in my mind so many times."

"The glitter ball falling?" I asked.

"Oh, no, not that, I didn't see that happen. I was... erm... I mean, I didn't stand still all night. I was working, not partying. So, no, I mean, I've replayed setting the glitter ball up."

"And?" I asked.

"I secured it the same way I always have. That glitter ball has been the main feature for years. And so, I'm thinking, did I just get complacent? But I honestly don't think I did. I remember fixing it up there like I always have. Trust me, that thing was pressure tested before I went ahead with it."

"I'm guessing it's pretty heavy?" I asked.

"Oh, no, it's not as heavy as it looks. Gosh, that sounds awful. It's too heavy to land on a person, obviously. But in terms of it staying up there, it's not that hard. Or at least, it shouldn't be."

"Do you think anyone imagines that you rigged the glitter ball on purpose to hurt Greasy?" I asked.

Lila gasped as she walked across to the kitchen table with a tray of hot chocolates and set them out in front of us.

"Are people saying that?" She asked.

"I don't know," I admitted.

"I don't see how that would even be possible. It's not as if it's on a timer or anything. How could I have made it drop at a certain time?"

"I don't know. I was just thinking how you said it's suspicious that it landed on your ex," I said.

"Oh, but there was no animosity between Lila and Greasy, dear," Mrs Claus said.

"No?" I asked. I should have guessed that in Candy Cane Hollow, even former partners still got on well. Was this place really real?

Lila shook her head but focused her gaze on her hot chocolate.

"But in theory, anyone could have got up that staircase to the ceiling beams? Or is it closed off?" I asked.

"It's not closed off. It's just a staircase, sometimes the teenagers go up there for a bit of privacy," Lila explained.

"You're really being very helpful, Lila," Mrs Claus reached across and gave her hand a squeeze.

"I am? I don't even know why you're asking these questions. Has someone accused me of something?"

"Oh, no. Although someone from Sleigh A While made a casual comment the other day about how you'd be the best person to rig a glitter ball," I said, then sat back and watched her reaction.

"Sleigh A While? Do you mean Drayton? He didn't say that, did he?"

"I've probably said too much," I took a long sip of the hot chocolate. It had a slight kick to it. Chilli, perhaps. It was delicious.

"I guess in theory I would be the best person, but I can't believe that anyone would imagine it was done deliberately. Is Wiggles treating this as a murder?"

"You'd have to ask Wiggles that," I said with a shrug.

"Do you think he should be treating it as a murder, dear?" Mrs Claus asked.

"There's no right answer, is there? Either I say it can't be a murder, and then I know my carelessness caused his death. Or I say it was murder and it just seems as though I'm trying to avoid responsibility."

"But what do you think, dear?"

Lila sighed. "I think I have to feed the reindeer now. And I also think I secured the glitter ball properly."

"Then it could be murder. If that's the case, Lila, help us. Who would want to kill Greasy?"

"He had a lot of enemies. He was a big character, always

saying whatever he wanted and not minding if it upset someone. Just last week he wrote that horrid article for the Chronicles about Peggy-Sue."

"What article?" I asked.

"That was him?" Mrs Claus asked at the same time.

"Peggy-Sue complains about everything, and she's always writing letters of complaint. Last week, there was an anonymous article complaining about her complaining, saying it was having a really bad impact on local businesses."

"And Greasy wrote that article?"

"It had to be him. Nobody else would dare, and I know his writing style. That's just one example of him upsetting someone. He didn't get along with Drayton, either, and I don't know why. They're both great chefs and foodies. They should have been friends, surely?"

"It sounds like Greasy could be stubborn," I suggested.

Lila rose from the table and went over to the cupboards, where she pulled out carrots and hunks of what looked like weeds. "You're welcome to stay, please don't think I'm being rude, but I have to get the food ready now."

"I think we'll be off now, dear," Mrs Claus said. We each drained the last of our hot chocolates and left Lila to her work, and her guilt.

## 9

The High Street was empty as we approached the GP surgery. The surgery was just as empty as the street and it needed to be inhabited again. It was such a feature of a small town, the GP surgery, and my heart sang as I looked at the building and considered that it could be my new workplace.

Mrs Claus had a set of skeleton keys for all of the businesses in Candy Cane Hollow and she unlocked the door and let us in.

"What did you think of Lila, dear?" Mrs Claus asked as she turned the dial on the radiator up and switched on the lights.

"She's not telling us everything," I said. I remembered how flustered she had grown at certain points of our conversation and wondered what she was hiding, or lying about.

"Does anyone? We all have our little secrets. Don't tell Father Christmas, but I'm a natural blonde," Mrs Claus said with a wink. I glanced at her white hair and smiled.

"Your secret's safe with me. What could Lila have as a secret, that's the question," I said, as I surveyed the space.

"All shall be revealed, I'm sure. Are you still believing that it was no accident?"

"Even more so. Watching Lila work, it's clear that she's very talented. If she's just a touch as talented in her events work, there's no way she would have made such a deadly mistake."

"I agree," Mrs Claus said.

"You do? That's brilliant. I'm so pleased to have someone on my side. Do you still want to help me investigate?"

"Of course, dear. What else do I have to keep me busy? Now, how about names for this place? I'm thinking of *Knock on Wood*."

"Really?" I asked, unsure whether a play on words was appropriate for a medical clinic.

"It's what you say when you're hoping you're well, isn't it? Knock on wood."

I shook my head a little and let out a laugh. "Knock on Wood. It has a certain ring to it. I'll need a receptionist."

"Of course. We should place an ad in the Chronicles and start the interviews right away," Mrs Claus beamed.

The bell rang out to signal that someone had come in the door, and we both turned to see Peggy-Sue in the doorway.

"Hello, dear," Mrs Claus greeted her.

"I saw the lights on."

"Yes, we're just starting to get this place ready for the new doctor," Mrs Claus said.

"It's taken too long. Over a week now, we've been without a doctor. It's not good enough," Peggy-Sue grumbled.

"Well, it was important to find the right person, not rush into anything. And the medics at the hospital are always just a phone call away."

"It's not the same. You won't get a bigwig hospital doctor looking at my bunions, I can tell you that for nothing. Who is he, then? The new doctor?"

I cleared my throat. "It's me. I'm Holly Wood."

"This is a joke, right?" Peggy-Sue eyed Mrs Claus.

"No, dear, Holly is a doctor. We're very lucky to find her," Mrs Claus said.

"Women are nurses. Men are doctors. Call me old-fashioned, but that's the way it is. Imagine I come in here with a bleeding head, she'd probably faint," Peggy-Sue looked at me with a sneer.

"I can assure you, I'm strong enough for this job. Both physically and mentally. And in my experience, it's the doctors who are shielded from some of those things more than the nurses."

Peggy-Sue shook her head. "I don't like it. I don't like it one bit. Next thing you'll be telling me your receptionist will be a man!"

"It will be whoever is the best person for the job," I said. I'd had several male receptionists over the years and had learned long ago that the only thing that mattered when judging a work colleague was their aptitude for the role. Could they calm down an irate patient? Could they handle a growing queue? Whether they were a Daniel or a Danielle made no difference in my book.

"It's all politically correct nonsense," Peggy-Sue said, then turned and stormed out of the surgery. Unfortunately, the door was one of those that moved incredibly slowly, so her attempts to bang it behind her were thwarted.

"She's a character," I said. I already had the sinking feeling that Peggy-Sue would be a frequent patient in the surgery. Every town had their difficult patients, even Candy Cane Hollow it appeared.

"Lonely, I think. She lives alone with her daughter. Will you change anything in here, dear?" Mrs Claus asked.

I considered the space and nodded. "A fresh coat of paint, just to freshen things up. I don't want to make it too different, because it's a space that people know. But a paint job would be good."

"Excellent! I'll help. We'll make quick work of it. Gilbert might even lend a hand, he's quite creative you know?"

"He is?"

"Oh, yes. Although he swore he hung up his paint-brushes when he came to work for us. I did encourage him to continue his art, but he swore he had no time for such foolish things anymore."

"That's intense," I said.

"I agree. But this project, as it's work, may just tempt him. He won't want to refuse a cry for help."

We finished up at the surgery, with Mrs Claus promising to call the sign maker, and plans made to begin painting the very next day.

By the time we locked up, the snow was really coming down, and I wished we had planned ahead and not set out on foot. As beautiful as the snowy landscape was, it was freezing.

No sooner had I finished that thought than a car beeped behind us, and we turned to see Wiggles inside his tiny Fiat, his favourite Christmas song playing on repeat as always.

"Hop in, ladies," he leaned over and called.

We dove into the car without an ounce of grace but with a huge amount of gratitude.

"Where can I take you fine ladies to?"

"Home, please. Have you had a busy day?"

Wiggles frowned. "I've been inundated with phone calls about Greasy's death."

"Really?" I asked, from the back seat.

He nodded. "Two people want to sue someone because when the glitter ball fell, shards of it tore holes in their clothes. Another got some dust on him and wants to be reimbursed for the dry cleaning. Four people rang in sick from work today because of the trauma of seeing the accident, and wanted me to sign their sick notes since we don't have a GP."

"We do have a GP, dear. Holly here will be getting set up at then surgery very soon," Mrs Claus said.

"Congratulations, Holly. I'm pleased to hear that. A lot of folks seem to think that if one emergency service isn't available, any of the others will do. But trust me, I know nothing about how to cure an ear ache."

"Wear earmuffs," Mrs Claus advised.

"Thank you, Mrs C, I'll forward the medical calls to you from now on," Wiggles said with a laugh so infectious we were soon all giggling away, until the chorus on his favourite song came on, at which point he insisted we all belt out the lyrics as loud as we could.

"Do you ever listen to anything else?" I asked, in the brief pause when the song ended and before it began again.

"Sure, I like to consider myself an open-minded kind of guy. A few years ago, I heard a different song. It was okay. Not bad at all."

I watched him closely for any signs of irony, but there was none.

"Wiggles, do you think Greasy's death might have been planned?" I asked.

"Of course not. The glitter ball fell and Greasy happened to be down there. It's a very tragic accident," Wiggles said. His head still bopped to the music as he spoke.

"Couldn't there be more to it than that?" I asked.

"I guess someone could have climbed up onto the beams, waited for the moment Greasy was in the right place, and then cut the glitter ball down. But, come on, it's not plausible really, is it?"

"Wiggles, you're a genius!"

"Erm, thanks?" He said with a chuckle.

"What is it, dear?" Mrs Claus asked from the front seat. She held her handbag on her lap and had reapplied her lipstick during the drive.

"I took photographs of the scene, just in case they might come in handy. I haven't even had chance to look at them. They might give us a clue," I explained as Wiggles stopped the car outside Claus Cottage.

"Well, I'll leave you ladies to your gruesome fun."

"Won't you come in, Wiggles? I'm sure Gilbert will have something tasty prepared."

"I'd love nothing more, but I'm on the way to make an arrest."

"What? You shouldn't have stopped to drive us if you were on important police business!" Mrs Claus scolded.

Wiggles laughed. "I always have a few minutes to spare to be chivalrous."

"Well, thank you."

"Who are you arresting?" I asked.

Wiggles shook his head. "I can't tell you that. What I can say is that it's not at all related to Greasy's death. Let's say that someone was seen selling shaved ice with a distinctly yellow tint."

"Eww! You're kidding!" I exclaimed.

"It's just a town kid pushing some boundaries," Wiggles said with a grin.

"And you're going to arrest him?"

"Her. And I won't actually do an arrest. Just turning up

in the old cop-mobile should make her think twice in future."

"Excellent thinking. These children nowadays, they really do get creative with their mischief!"

"I probably did worse as a youngster," Wiggles admitted.

"Me too," I mumbled. I'd had a few years of systematically ignoring all good advice while acting silly and trying to impress the wrong people.

"I was quite the good girl," Mrs Claus said. There was a sparkle in her eyes and I wasn't sure I believed her.

"Of course," Wiggles said, but he turned in his seat a little and gave me a wink.

"We'd better let you be on your way," Mrs Claus said. She leaned in and planted a kiss on his cheek, and we forced ourselves out of the tiny vehicle. As soon as we'd closed the doors, we heard Wiggles turn the music up and begin to sing along.

We stood on the doorstep and watched as his tiny car drove away.

"You were a good girl?" I asked with a smile.

Mrs Claus beamed at me. "Or perhaps I just never got caught!"

## 10

The next day, we were up and out early.

Mrs Claus and Gilbert went ahead to Knock on Wood to lay dust sheets and give the walls a clean, while Nick and I went into town to choose paint.

It was the first chance I'd had to spend any time alone with Nick since the Ball, and I found that I felt nervous.

We drove across town mainly in silence, each of us humming along to the radio and lost in our own thoughts.

I wondered if Nick had realised that he just wanted us to be friends. Maybe he was having doubts. Maybe he wanted me to leave Candy Cane Hollow and return to my old life in London.

"You're quiet," he said as he found a space in the car park of Joseph's Technicolour Paint Shop.

"So are you," I said. My words came out harder than I planned, and I winced.

"I guess a lot's happened," he said with a smile. The dimple in his cheek taunted me. I wished I could reach out and stroke it, but I didn't have the courage.

"You're right. Look, I know you're busy. You don't have to

help with this," I said. If Nick Claus was having doubts, I wanted to let him off the hook easily.

"Never too busy to be chivalrous," Nick murmured.

I cocked my head to one side. "Wiggles said the same thing. Do they teach that in school here?"

"Not quite. It's an important part of our culture here, though."

I sighed. "There's so much to learn."

"Are you sure this is what you want? Leaving your big fancy London life behind and moving here?" Nick asked. Here it was, the chance for me to disappear and make it easy for him to believe it was my decision all along.

But that willingness to disappear, to not reply to a message or return a call, was probably a good part of why I had been single for so long. I saw the potential for a good thing and got scared.

What would happen if I was honest instead?

"I'm not sure how everything will work out, Nick, but I want to give it a try and find out," I said.

Nick swallowed and I felt the awkwardness in the car with us. My heart thumped in my chest. What was he going to say?

"I feel guilty at times," he finally said.

"Guilty for what?" I asked, and a thought played out in my head. What if Nick was about to confess to killing Greasy? I shook my head. That was nonsense. I was getting carried away with the whole amateur sleuth thing.

"You have a life in London. A family, friends too I'm sure. A home. I wonder if it's fair to ask you to give all of that up," he met my gaze and offered a sad smile.

"Nick, I want to be here. I'm ready for a change. And I'm excited - and terrified - to see what happens between us, but I'm not making this decision just for that reason. I've never been welcomed anywhere the way I've been welcomed here. I don't think it would be possible for me to leave now and return to my old life."

He smiled. "Really?"

"I promise. I'm not the kind of woman who drops everything for a man, even a man as amazing as Santa," I said with a laugh.

"I know that. Trust me, I do. I've been the most eligible bachelor in Candy Cane Hollow, just because of my job title. It's been hard to know whether interest has been in me or the red suit, you know?"

"I understand that a little bit. There's an awkward point on a first date where I have to reveal that I'm a doctor, and everything changes at that point. Some guys really like the status of that, and others are really scared by it. Either way, I stop just being Holly when I tell them."

"I'm not scared by it," he murmured.

"No?" I asked. I couldn't meet his gaze. The inside of the car was suddenly really hot and the windows had steamed up.

"I think it's really cool. Next time you give me concussion in a snowball fight, you can at least tend to my injuries," he said with a laugh.

The ice broken, I pushed open the door and found myself walking out into yet another snowstorm. Nick came around to my side of the car, grabbed my hand, and we made a run for it together.

The paint shop was tiny, one of a row of old fashioned stores, and it seemed that we were the only customers in the place.

A wizened old elf sat on a stool behind the till, his attention focused on a paperback book that looked as old as him.

"What kind of colour are you thinking?" Nick asked.

"Something cheerful and bright. Maybe a yellow or a green." I said.

We walked the aisles, each of us picking up shade cards and studying the colours on them.

"They even do glitter paint, no way!" Nick exclaimed.

I looked over at him and laughed. "That could be fun."

In the end, we settled on a pale yellow shade and paid at the counter. Nick insisted on carrying the paint and we made a mad dash across the car park back to the dry safety of Nick's car.

"I've been thinking of asking you out. On a second date. Would that be okay?" Nick asked as he started the engine.

I tried to play it cool but couldn't stop the grin. "That would be more than okay!"

"Phew. You've been so busy since the Ball, I was starting to think maybe you were avoiding me."

My stomach flipped as I realised how my busybody sleuthing might have appeared to him.

"I'm sorry. I've been trying to give you space. You must be so busy."

"Never too busy..."

"... to be chivalrous?" I finished.

"That, yes. But also, never too busy for the people who matter. Being Santa is pretty intense, that's true, but the best Santas are the ones who make their loved ones feel special, not just the children of the world."

I swallowed. "Loved ones?"

He reached across and squeezed my hand, and we continued the journey in a comfortable silence. The car wipers worked quickly to try and clear the snow as it fell, and the radio was playing carols on a low volume.

We reached Knock on Wood far too quickly for my

liking, and burst into the surgery with our paint and brushes.

"Excellent, you made it. The snow's really coming down out there! We'll make quick work of this, dear," Mrs Claus gushed as Nick and I stomped the snow off of our boots on the welcome mat.

Gilbert had changed into a skin-tight black onesie and was wearing protective eyewear.

"Goodness gumdrops, are you painting or preparing for an extreme sport?" I teased.

He gave a sarcastic laugh. "Mock me now, Holly Wood, but you'll wish you'd planned ahead when your clothes are ruined by paint splatters."

"I'm just pleased he's not naked," Nick said with a wink.

"You couldn't handle that," Gilbert said with a sashay of his tiny body.

"Oh, I couldn't. I know that!"

"Less chat and more work. Some of us have got lunch to prepare after this," Gilbert chastised us.

We each picked up a paintbrush and began working on a different wall. It was clear that Gilbert was being competitive, speed-painting his way around a whole wall in the time it took me to try and do neat edging.

"It's not a race, dear," Mrs Claus warned him.

Gilbert snickered at us. Maybe he was getting a little high on the paint fumes.

"Shall I finish your wall?" Gilbert asked Nick.

"I'm doing okay, thanks. Why don't you start in the other room?" Nick suggested.

"No problemo," Gilbert agreed. He stood on the tips of his toes and did a little victory dance, and we could all see what was going to happen before it did.

I opened my mouth to warn him, but he tripped on an

uneven section of the dust sheet and tumbled, falling backwards into the can of paint, where he sat, his slight frame a perfect fit into the large can.

"Oh, I say!" Mrs Claus giggled.

"Well don't just stand and watch, get me out of here!" Gilbert exclaimed.

We all climbed up from the floor. Mrs Claus and I grabbed a hand of his each while Nick held on to the paint can.

"One, two, three," we said in unison, and then we pulled the little elf out of the can. The jolt left us all splattered with yellow paint, but it was Gilbert who came off worst, a proud yellow circle painted over his bottom.

"This goes no further than this room, do you understand?" Gilbert said, and we nodded our agreement even as we stifled our laughter.

## 11

With the painting finished, and Gilbert's onesie on a high temperature wash, we each went off to a different bathroom and scrubbed ourselves clean.

I had splatters of paint on my hands, my arms, in my hair and even one bit on my teeth.

I enjoyed a long, hot shower and then inspected myself in the mirror until I was happy that I'd found every spot of paint and got rid of it.

Dried and dressed, I made my way down to the kitchen, where Gilbert was back in his usual working attire. It was hard to believe that he'd ever dressed in the skintight lycra, or fallen into a pot of paint, and yet I knew we'd never let him live the incident down.

"I suppose you're on the hunt for food?" Gilbert asked.

"Not unless you're making something," I said.

"Of course I'm making something. What kind of establishment do you think this is? The kind where you come in and open the cupboards yourself, in the hope that a scrap of food remains? I've made soup. Soup and homemade ciabatta," Gilbert said with a flourish.

I thought I saw a discarded plastic wrapper on the side, and couldn't believe that Gilbert had had time to prepare his own bread, but I decided to let it go. He was having a bad enough day without me catching him out with a culinary shortcut.

Mrs Claus joined us in the kitchen and explained that Nick had been called away to deal with a toy emergency down at the HQ.

She joined me at the table and we gratefully devoured the soup and bread. It turned out, we were so tired from the painting that we didn't have any energy to tease Gilbert about the paint escapades.

"What are you doing for the rest of the day, Holly?" Mrs Claus asked.

"I need to look at the photos from the Ball," I said.

"Ooh! Can I look with you?"

"Sure," I agreed, and we stacked our empty bowls in the middle of the table, and thanked Gilbert for a tasty lunch.

"Oh, Gilbert, dear. Careful you don't fall into the soup pan," Mrs Claus called as we left the room.

Gilbert huffed and clattered around by way of response, and we stifled our laughter as we walked across into the den.

The fire was roaring in there and I stood in front of it for a few moments to soak up some heat. My feet in particular had never known cold like in Candy Cane Hollow. I would have to invest in some really chunky socks and a pair of slippers too. Maybe even a spare pair for my new surgery!

I'd transferred the photos from my phone to my laptop, and I set the device up on the coffee table and opened the folder where I'd stored them.

"So, here we go. I took some photographs before the glitter ball fell. I'll flick through them," I said.

There was a photo of Mrs Claus and Father Christmas, both of them beaming from ear to ear.

"Goodness, doesn't he look handsome? I swear he hasn't aged a day!" Mrs Claus gushed as she eyed up her husband on the screen.

Then there was a selfie of me and Nick, and he was gazing at me with so much devotion that I felt my cheeks flame. I could tell that Mrs Claus was desperate to make some comment about the picture, but she managed to hold her tongue.

There were general shots of the venue, of the group gathered for the Ball, and on one photo I spotted what must be the staircase up to the beams.

"I think that's how you get up to the ceiling," I tapped the screen.

"It is, dear, yes. You think someone used those stairs?"

"It seems like the only option really. Unless someone rigged the glitter ball before it was fixed up there."

"I'm no technophobe but I can't see how that would be possible," Mrs Claus said.

I smiled at her mistaken use of the word technophobe. "I can't, either."

I flicked to the next image. Another general scene, showing the Candy Cane Hollow residents laughing and chatting.

"There's someone by the staircase, dear. Look," Mrs Claus said.

I picked up the laptop and gazed at the image. She was right. Near the staircase was a man on his own, and the image had caught him clearly mid-stride. He was approaching the staircase.

I felt my heartbeat race as I realised who the man in the image was.

"It's Drayton," I murmured.

"It certainly is," Mrs Claus agreed.

I carried on flicking through the images, but the next ones I'd taken didn't show the staircase at all.

Finally, I got to the images I had taken after the glitter ball had fallen.

"These pictures are quite gruesome. Are you ready?" I warned.

Mrs Claus looked at me with a steely gaze and nodded.

As soon as I flicked to the next image, she gasped and began to cry, but insisted I keep going.

The shots of Greasy under the glitter ball gave us no help. He was clearly dead, but there was nothing else to be discovered from looking at him.

I flicked past and reached the image I had hoped for. It showed the top of the glitter ball, including the fixings that should have kept it hovering above the dance floor.

I studied the image and clapped my hands together.

"Look at this. This is the clip that fastens the glitter ball up there."

"I can see it, dear," Mrs Claus said.

"Someone went up there and unclipped it. We're right, there is foul play here!"

"I'm not sure I follow, dear."

"Look how the clip has come down? It's not damaged, and the chain links that connect the glitter ball to the clip are all intact. If the ball had collapsed under the weight, the links would have torn or the clip would have come down with part of the ceiling attached to it."

Mrs Claus gasped. "Someone's just unfastened the clip and let it fall? Oh my. Goodness gumdrops."

"You can say that again," I murmured.

"What do we do now?"

"I'm going to go and speak to Wiggles. Once he sees this evidence, he's going to have to investigate," I said.

"Good idea!" Mrs Claus exclaimed, then her brow furrowed.

"What's wrong?"

"I just realised that I have a meeting with the Natter & Knit ladies."

"Oh, that's okay. You go and do that and I'll speak to Wiggles."

"I can go via Candy Cane Custody and drop you off?" Mrs Claus offered.

I accepted the offer of a lift to protect my poor cold feet from more walking through the snow.

We pulled up outside the police station and I bid farewell to Mrs Claus, took a deep breath and pushed open the door to the foyer.

I was always pleasantly surprised by how festive the place was, with its huge real Christmas tree and the festive tunes playing out.

Wiggles was right there in front of me, and who was with him but Peggy-Sue.

"I demand an investigation!" She screeched.

"Now, now, I can't say that I imagine there was any dishonesty intended," Wiggles said.

"What would you call it, then?"

"Run it by me again," Wiggles asked as he scratched his head.

"It says clear as day, right here on the packaging: contains at least 12 baubles!" Peggy-Sue raised an eyebrow as if her case had been proven with that one sentence.

"And?"

"And this package contained 12 baubles exactly."

"I just don't see what the issue is," Wiggles admitted.

"At least 12 baubles suggests more than 12! It's false advertising! These enormous companies have to be controlled or they'll take liberty after liberty. I'll bet if I go back and buy more, every single pack will include no more than 12 baubles. In which case, the description should be 12 baubles. The suggestion of more than 12 doesn't need to be made!"

"Okay. I'll file a report and see what we can do," Wiggles agreed, defeated.

"Thank you," Peggy-Sue said. She turned and saw me out of the corner of her eye and scowled at me.

"I'll wait," I said with a smile, and sank into one of the plush chairs in the foyer.

"Of course you will, you arrived after me. I see you're one of those people who thinks your status means you should automatically go to the front of the queue," Peggy-Sue said.

"Not at all, I'm happy to wait," I said. I'd actually never used my doctor status to my benefit. If anything, the title embarrassed me at times and I often hid it.

"Good. Because I'm here on important business," Peggy-Sue said.

"Let's get these details down. You say this is an issue with an enormous company? Which one are we talking about?" Wiggles asked, pen poised by his notepad.

"I bought them from Bruce's."

"Bruce's Bauble Emporium?" Wiggles returned his pen to the counter and rubbed his temple.

"That's the place. You're familiar with it because he's been up to no good before, I take it?"

"I'm familiar with it because I buy my new baubles there every year," Wiggles admitted.

"Ah, I see. But can you investigate him fairly?"

"Peggy, listen..."

"It's Peggy-Sue," she corrected.

"Sorry, my bad. Listen, Bruce is a one man band. He's not out to mislead anyone. He'll have counted these baubles in the pack by hand."

"I'm not challenging his ability to count. I want the description changing," Peggy-Sue insisted.

Wiggles sighed. "I'll go and make a couple of phone calls. Wait here."

He disappeared from the counter and Peggy-Sue paced the foyer.

"We have to stand up against these titans of industry," she muttered.

It sounded like Bruce wasn't a titan of anything, but I didn't want to get involved.

Suddenly, she stopped pacing and glared across at me.

"What are you here for, anyway?"

"Oh, I have to talk to Wiggles about something," I said.

"Hmm. I guess you're aware that The Greasy Spoon is re-opening?"

"Twisty said he planned to re-open, yes," I said.

"It'll be a better place without Greasy," Peggy-Sue said.

"You didn't get along with him, did you?"

"I didn't enjoy his cooking. There's a difference. I had no opinion about the man behind the ketchup."

"But he wrote that article about you," I said.

Her eye twitched a little. "What article?"

"The one in the Chronicles, about the effect your complaints are having on businesses."

She scoffed. "I don't read that rag."

"Really? But you have letters published in it quite often." I asked.

"I write to the place. That doesn't mean I read it. I had no idea that Greasy had taken to writing about me. I shall have to request a back copy and inspect his work, I expect his grammar to be as sloppy as his food hygiene," Peggy-Sue said.

"I'm not sure that's a good idea. I think the letter was pretty scathing. Are you sure you haven't heard about it before?"

"Absolutely not. I remember everything," she said.

"Do you remember how awful it was when the glitter ball fell?" I asked, hoping the sudden change of subject would catch her unawares.

She scoffed. "I wasn't there to see. I was discussing an important matter with Mrs Claus."

"You were?"

"The toilets that night were disgusting. I have no idea who was on the cleaning team but they did a shoddy job. I felt a matter of hygiene should be escalated to the highest authority, so I found Mrs Claus and reported it to her."

"Right at the time that Greasy died?"

"Yes. And do you know the amazing thing? I was the only person to mention the toilets! It made me question whether anyone else in Candy Cane Hollow cares about cleanliness. I've been extra careful to sterilise my hands since then, I can tell you."

"I can imagine. So if someone has a grudge against Greasy, it wouldn't be you?" I pushed.

"Of course not. It would be Lila. She's furious with him for their break up. I overheard her sobbing about it on the night of the Ball. And then, of course, there would be Drayton."

My ears pricked up at the name of the man who had been near the staircase. "Drayton?"

"He wants Sleigh A While to be the venue of choice in town, and his menu is certainly the classier affair. But Greasy had this strange appeal with people. Drayton wanted Greasy out of the way."

Wiggles returned to the desk and cleared his throat.

"All sorted, I hope?" Peggy-Sue asked.

"I made the call but there was no answer. I'll give Bruce the opportunity to explain his side of things and then make a decision," Wiggles explained.

"Really? You're not sending a squad car out to arrest him right away? What else do you have to deal with?"

"Well, I'm practicing for the Figure Skating competition," Wiggles said with a smile.

Peggy-Sue scowled at him.

"Work-wise you mean? I can't possibly disclose that information. But leave it with me!"

Peggy-Sue huffed her way out of the police station and I watched as she immediately squeezed some antibacterial gel on her hands after touching the door.

"Please don't tell me that you're here about an odd number of leaves on your poinsettia plant or some other nonsense like that?" Wiggles pleaded with me.

"Afraid not. I really need to talk to you about Greasy's death," I said.

"What about it?"

"He was murdered. I'm certain of it."

Wiggles let out a long breath, as if I'd just made a bad day even worse. "You'd better come through."

He buzzed me through the door to the inner workings of the police station.

I followed him to his office, a cubby-hole of a room with an MDF desk and a small window looking out over Candy Cane Hollow.

I lowered myself carefully into the spare plastic chair. The rest of the decor inside Candy Cane Custody was plush and welcoming, and even the rooms inside the jail itself were more like a 4-star hotel.

Wiggles must have seen the surprise on my face because he said, "I've never felt right spending police money on my own room. This furniture was all here when I took over the role and it's done me fine. A police officer should be out and about anyway, not holed up in their own office. Now, about this potential murder?"

I reached into my bag and pulled out my phone.

"You'll probably remember that I took photos that night? Well, this one shows the clip of the glitter ball. It's not damaged. None of the chain links are damaged."

Wiggles leaned in and looked at the image. "That's curious."

I flicked to the next image. "And here's the staircase that goes up to the ceiling. Take a look and see who's about to go up there."

"Is that Drayton?" Wiggles asked.

I nodded. "He never liked Greasy. He wanted to put him out of business. Plus, the man's awful. I had to get Mrs Claus involved in the way he was treating a female member of staff recently."

"You went straight to Mrs Claus?"

"Well, I rang her to vent really and she insisted on dealing with it."

Wiggles chuckled. "Of course she did. Well, I can't charge a man with murder because he was seen near a staircase. You know that, right?"

I felt the disappointment twist in my stomach. Of course being near a staircase wasn't strong enough evidence.

"But I think you could be onto something, Holly. You're

right that that chain should have been damaged if it had collapsed under the weight."

"Really?" I asked with a smile.

"It's worth taking a look at. Good thing you took those photographs. I was ready to write it off as a tragic accident. You've got a good instinct for these things."

"Thank you!" I gushed.

Wiggles glanced at his watch and rose from his own plastic chair.

"Where are we going? Are we going to speak to Drayton now?" I felt the adrenaline flood through my body.

"Now? Goodness gumdrops, no. I have a rehearsal to get to," Wiggles said.

"Rehearsal?"

"For the Figure Skating competition."

"I thought that was a joke," I admitted.

Wiggles looked down at his rotund shape and then raised an eyebrow at me. "This right here is the physique of an athlete on the ice. But don't worry, I'll go and speak to Drayton soon. Tomorrow afternoon, perhaps."

I felt myself exhale with relief. "Thank you. I appreciate it."

## 12

The thing I had learned about calling a very cold place home was that it created an appreciation for warmth. Any time I could close the door, light a fire, put on slippers, or slide under a blanket, it felt like a real luxury.

And that's why I had no intention of waking up.

"Holly, come on," the voice repeated.

I closed my eyes tight and willed myself back to sleep. Whoever that velvet voice belonged to, they had stumbled into the wrong bedroom at the wrong time.

"It's important. I know you can hear me. Come on, open those eyes," the voice continued.

It was a delicious voice. The kind of voice that could tell me a bedtime story for the rest of my life. But even that kind of voice had no place interrupting the warm cocoon of my sleep.

"No!" I mumbled as I pulled the covers over my head.

"Baby, you'll want to wake up. Trust me," the voice came again. Insistent little delicious voice, it was.

"Never," I said.

I had never been a morning person, which made my career choice ridiculous. Becoming a GP had at least removed the ungodly shift patterns and on call rota from my life, but I'd done enough of them while training.

In Candy Cane Hollow my attachment to my bed and my precious sleep schedule had grown. It was just so cold outside of the blankets.

The voice sighed and I felt the pressure from where they had perched on the end of the bed ease. They were going away. I had fought the battle of my right to sleep in, and won!

"I didn't want to have to do this, but it's time for the ice cold water. That's the best way to wake up a sleeping beauty," the voice said.

I jumped up and peeled my eyes open, then glared at Nick, who was stood at the side of my bed.

He smiled at me and that irresistible dimple greeted me good morning too.

"What are you doing here? You've never come into my bedroom before," I asked as the reality of the situation sank in.

He sat back down on the bed and reached for my hands. "Holly, something's happened. Wiggles has just called. There's been a second death."

"No!" I cried.

"It's true."

"Who?"

"Come on, get dressed and I'll take you to the station. Wiggles is going to interview the person who found the body and he said he'd appreciate your help."

"He did?" I asked in disbelief. I jumped out of bed and quickly washed, dressed and smoothed down my hair.

We rode across town and I felt jittery with nerves the whole way.

"Do I look okay? Is this outfit right to interrogating a murder suspect?" I asked as we pulled outside Candy Cane Custody.

Nick looked me up and down and gave me a smile of approval. I'd gone for muted colours and something that approached professional, which wasn't easy since my Candy Cane Hollow wardrobe mainly consisted of Christmas jumpers and everything in red and green.

"You look perfect. I'm not sure this is an interrogation, though. This is the person who found the body, remember. You'll do great," Nick said.

He leaned across and planted a kiss on my cheek.

I felt my skin flush. I felt as nervous as if I was being dropped off for my first day at a new job.

I took a breath, got out of the car, and made my way into the police station.

At the reception desk was an elf who looked young enough to still be in school. His face was covered with angry-looking acne and he was fixing jewels to a piece of fabric with a hot glue gun as I entered.

"Good morning, I'm here to see Wiggles," I said with a shaky smile. In the battle between me and my nerves, my nerves were winning.

"Chief Superintendent Wiggles?"

"Yes, that's him! He's asked for me. I'm Holly. Holly Wood."

"Holly Wood? That's an alias, right?"

"No, no, it's my real name," I said.

The youth raised an eyebrow. "You're telling me that your real name is Holly Wood?"

"That's right. It's really quite urgent that I speak to Wiggles."

"He's in an interview. But let's get back to your name. You do realise that this is a police station? We have records on everyone. I can zap your fingerprint right now and find out your real name," the elf said.

"Erm, actually you can't because I've never had my fingerprints taken so I won't be on your database," I said.

"Everyone's in the database," he said.

"Only the people who've had their DNA taken for some reason," I insisted.

He frowned and placed his glue gun down on the counter. "Is that true? I'm sure it's everyone. My Aunt Doreen's on there."

"Well, I could be wrong," I backtracked.

"Goodness gumdrops! Are you telling me that Auntie Doreen is a criminal?"

"No!" I exclaimed, but he was typing manically on his computer.

He hit the Return key and waited a moment, then gasped. "She was interviewed! She was accused of being a serial... a serial..."

I really wanted to get to Wiggles but I also really wanted to hear what nasty business Auntie Doreen had got herself mixed up with.

"A serial litterer!" The elf finally exclaimed. His face had drained of colour. Auntie Doreen had just brought shame on his family.

"Well, if she was just interviewed, that means she was innocent, right? Or she'd have been charged and locked up!" I said with a smile.

The elf shook his blemished face and grabbed his glue gun again. "There's no smoke without fire. That's what I say.

I'll be having words with Auntie Doreen, you can bet your last icicle on that. She always has been a bit wild and free with her refuse disposal - leaves her rubbish bin outside for days after it's been emptied, she does!"

"I'm sure a chat will help you get to the bottom of it. Can you buzz me through to see Wiggles now, please?"

"Oh no. He's in an interview. I said that already," the elf said. His attention had returned to his crystals.

"He needs me in that interview. He's specifically requested that I come over and assist him," I said in my most stern voice. I usually saved that voice for consultants who refused to take patient referrals from me. It always worked.

"No can do, sorry. I never interrupt an interview," he said. He was clearly made of tougher stuff than NHS consultants were.

I resisted the temptation to lean over and threaten him with his own glue gun, and instead began to pace the foyer, until an idea emerged.

"Did you ever read the case papers about that serial litterer?" I asked.

"What do you mean?" He asked. He laid the glue gun down and I had his attention. Luckily, everyone in Candy Cane Hollow loved gossip.

"I heard that they never felt they'd got the right person. I was just thinking, maybe it was Auntie Doreen after all," I shrugged my shoulders.

He practically flew out of his chair and out of sight in search of the case archives.

I approached the reception desk and checked that nobody else was around, then pulled myself up and over. On the other side of the desk, I was free to explore the inner workings of the police station.

Unfortunately, the place was like a labyrinth. Corridor after corridor stretched out as if for miles, and I had no idea where to find Wiggles.

I noticed a uniformed police officer ahead of me and decided to try some false bravado.

"Excuse me, Constable. Can you point me towards the interview that Chief Superintendent Wiggles is conducting?"

The officer looked me up and down and I was grateful for my sombre clothes.

"Follow me, ma'am," he said.

He lead me on an intricate path of lefts, rights, and two security locked doors that I'd have had no chance of getting past unaccompanied.

Eventually, he gave a short rap on the door of Interview C4, then pushed the heavy door open.

Wiggles looked up at me and gave a slight smile.

"Thank you," I said to the officer.

He grinned at me. "I don't know how you broke in here, but I figured Wiggles could deal with you. I'll leave you to it."

My cheeks flamed but I entered the room and heard it clunk closed behind me.

In the interview room were two plush chairs and, across from them, a luxurious sofa. I sat in the chair next to Wiggles and finally looked across to see who we were about to interview.

## 13

"I've read Peggy-Sue her rights, although of course she's here as a witness and isn't under suspicion at this stage," Wiggles said, for my benefit.

"At this stage?!" Peggy-Sue exclaimed from the settee. She looked tiny sitting there, and the fear was written across her face.

"I have to phrase it that way," Wiggles said with a smile.

"Hmm. What's she doing here, anyway?" Peggy-Sue eyed me with suspicion. I didn't blame her. Why had Wiggles asked me to join him?

"Holly here will be assisting in the enquiries. In fact, I have some papers I have to read through, so she may lead the interview after I've done the first few questions."

I glanced at the papers on his lap and read the heading.

*Advanced Figure Skating Rules & Regulations, Updated Edition Version 7.4a*

I raised an eyebrow.

"I'll set the scene, for the benefit of the tape. Around 5.45 this morning, Candy Cane Custody received a phone call from yourself, Peggy-Sue, advising that you had found a dead body. We attended the scene and did, indeed, see the body of Twisty Rumples. Can you start by talking us through what happened?"

Twisty was dead?

I felt stunned by the news. I thought that Greasy's death had been suspicious, but Twisty dying just days afterwards surely made it clear to everyone that they were both murders and must be linked.

Who would want both Greasy and Twisty dead?

"I was out walking and I saw a figure crumpled on the ground outside Sleigh A While. I thought perhaps it was a drunk at first and I wondered what Candy Cane Hollow was turning into, but as I got closer I recognised him," Peggy-Sue said. Her voice was firm and judgemental, even as she described the poor man's death.

"Early to be out walking, no?" Wiggles asked.

"I have the same route and I take it at the same time each day. I enjoy the quiet. I also like to see how the town looks each day. It's amazing what you can see at that time. You may recall that just a month ago I filed a report about several businesses keeping their interior lights on all night? I queried the waste of electricity. Well, I made that discovery on a morning walk," Peggy-Sue said with pride.

"You're being a good neighbour filing all of these reports, aren't you?" I asked, as I realised just how she saw the role she was playing.

"Of course. Someone has to monitor the standards we are setting for ourselves, and since nobody else seems to care quite as much as I do, I've taken on the job. It's unpaid, unpopular, but vital."

"And we thank you. Now, returning to this morning. Did Twisty speak to you? Make any noises at all?" Wiggles asked.

Peggy-Sue glared across at him. "He was dead."

"You know that how? Did you check for a pulse, or..."

"Well, no, no I didn't. I didn't lay a finger on him. I thought it pretty obvious from the state of him."

"And you called the police right away when you found him?" I asked. Wiggles had picked up his papers and began to read them with deep concentration. It seemed that I was on my own, investigating a murder. Be careful what you wish for, as they say.

"I did. What else would I do? I was very conscious that this scene was right there on the High Street. It's bad for business. Bad for morale! The mess had to be cleared away."

"The mess? That mess was a person," I said quietly.

"Exactly. Was. Used to be. When I came across him, he was already dead and gone and the High Street was no place for him."

"Did you see anyone else around?" I asked.

"I don't recall. I wasn't paying attention before coming across his body."

"So you didn't see anything suspicious?"

"I saw a dead body, I'd say that was plenty of suspicious things to see first thing in the morning. Clearly, he was killed! Clearly, whoever killed Greasy decided to kill Twisty too. So you're looking for a person with a reason to want them both dead."

"Thank you for that," I said with a thin smile.

"It's really not my job to spell it out for you, but it seems fairly straightforward," Peggy-Sue said.

"Do you have any ideas who could have wanted them both dead?" I asked. I guessed that Peggy-Sue was a woman with an opinion on everything.

"Of course I do. It's Drayton, isn't it? He wanted The

Greasy Spoon closed down and he's got what he wanted now, hasn't he!"

"It's a bit drastic, isn't it? Killing the competition?" I asked, even though I agreed that he was the main suspect.

"There's the woman involved too. That complicated everything, doesn't it?" Peggy-Sue asked.

"What woman?"

"Greasy's ex. The one who does the events."

"Lila? What about her?" I asked.

"She was all over Drayton at the Ball. I saw them kissing at one point. And not the way you'd kiss your grandfather, if you know what I mean. A disgusting public display of affection. Save it for indoors, I say."

"You saw Lila and Drayton kissing at the Ball?" I asked.

"Yes, down by the toilets. No doubt they were so carried away with passion that they didn't care who saw."

"That's interesting. You really are being very helpful, Peggy-Sue."

"At this stage, we believe that Twisty was trampled by a reindeer," Wiggles glanced up from his paperwork to add that. It was genius, really. It looked as if he was reading a formal report about Twisty's death, not revising for his figure skating competition.

My mind flashed back to Drayton's warning. He'd threatened to crush the competition. Could that really be a coincidence?

"Did you see any reindeer around?" I asked.

Peggy-Sue considered the question and shook her head. "None nearby. I'd know because I have allergies, you see. I'd have felt if one was close."

"Allergic to reindeer? That's got to make life fun in Candy Cane Hollow," I said with a smile.

"Is that relevant? I'm not here to talk about my

personal lived experience of Candy Cane Hollow, or as an allergy-sufferer. Keep your questions focused, please."

I narrowed my eyes a little. Fine. If she wanted to play mean, I could do the same.

"How do you feel about the fact that you've been implicated by another person involved in this investigation?" I asked.

Peggy-Sue's face turned an impossible shade of crimson and she grabbed her snowman-shaped handbag and clutched it to her.

"How dare you suggest such a thing? I demand a full explanation," she said.

"I'm not able to reveal all of the details at this stage, but I can say that you were named as a person who may have had a grudge against Greasy," I said.

"Greasy! What's he got to do with this? I'm talking about Twisty and I never had a single issue with him!"

"But you did have an issue with Greasy?"

"With his cooking! With his food hygiene levels! I wouldn't have wasted my time fraternising with a man who only owned one cutting board. Every food professional should know the different colour cutting boards and follow that system. What if I have a celery allergy and celery is the thing he chopped before he chopped whatever I ordered?" Peggy-Sue ranted.

"The person who named you said that you were furious about the letter he wrote to the Chronicles about you," I said.

"And I've already told you that I knew nothing about that weak attempt at writing."

"And you know nothing about a reindeer trampling Twisty to death?"

"I know how the aftermath of it looked, that's as much as I can help you with."

"You couldn't have been responsible for that reindeer?"

"Absolutely not. I have no experience with reindeer. My allergies wouldn't let me near one."

"I think that's all that I have to ask you for now," I said. Wiggles gave me a slight nod to indicate that he agreed.

WE LOITERED in the interview room after Peggy-Sue had left. It was a more comfortable space and closer to the kitchen, where Wiggles disappeared off to and returned with a hot chocolate for each of us.

"I can't believe that Twisty's been killed," I said.

"Me either. I wish I'd gone out and spoke to Drayton last night, Holly. It's just... this competition, I'm not getting any younger and this might be my last chance to compete at this level," Wiggles explained.

"I understand. You have a right to a personal life. Maybe I could help?"

"Help? You figure skate?"

"Oh, goodness, no! I meant maybe I could help with the investigation? I can interview people for you, or with you. I think it's clear that Drayton needs speaking to next."

Wiggles laughed. "Oh, right, yes! Help with the investigation. That would be great. Drayton's our man, you think?"

"I'm not sure. Everything seems to be pointing to him, but is it all too neat and tidy?"

"It would be a clumsy killer who left a body right outside their own business," Wiggles agreed.

"Unless he hopes that by making it so obvious we actually suspect him less," I said.

"Good point."

"If it is him, I wouldn't be surprised if he tries to make a run for it," I said.

Wiggles carefully placed his hot chocolate on the table and gazed at me. "We'd better get after him then."

## 14

W e sped across town in Wiggles' tiny Fiat with Last Christmas on repeat, and I found that the car felt a bit more comfortable, as if my body was beginning to adjust to the cramped space and the familiar grooves of the seat.

The lights were on inside Sleigh A While but the door was closed and locked.

Wiggles thudded on the door.

"Police, open up!" He called.

A few moments passed, and then the door was opened. Drayton's skin tone was almost grey it was so pale. He looked exhausted, like a very ill man or father of a newborn baby.

"I've been expecting you," he said. He let us in, then peered out of the door and bolted it behind him.

Inside the bistro, two suitcases were open on the floor, each one half-full.

"What's going on?" Wiggles asked.

"I'm not staying here! Someone's targeting the food industry! It'll be me they're after next!"

"You mean you're leaving because you don't feel safe?" I asked.

"Of course! Why is that surprising?"

"It's surprising because you're under suspicion," I said.

He cackled. "Me? A murderer? You must be having a laugh."

"We don't find murder a very funny thing, actually," Wiggles said.

"Well, no, of course not. You know what I'm saying."

"Where were you between the hours of 5am and 6am today?" I asked.

He rolled his eyes. "In bed. Asleep. Alone."

"No witnesses, then?"

"I don't typically sleep with a roomful of witnesses, no."

"Nobody could confirm where you were right at the moment of Greasy dying either. That's an unfortunate coincidence," I said.

He shook his head and continued piling things into the suitcases. "I do have an alibi for the Ball. I was trying to be respectful not sharing it."

"Go on, then. What is it?"

"I was snogging the face off of Greasy's ex-girlfriend if you really want to know. The commotion when the glitter ball fell was the only thing that stopped us," Drayton said.

"You were kissing Lila?"

"Is that her name?"

I frowned.

"What? I barely know the girl and I can't say we spent any time talking that night. She's not up to my normal standards but she was a decent kisser, actually. Sometimes it works that way. The really drop dead gorgeous ones don't need to put as much effort in."

"You really are a charmer," I snapped. He was intolerable. If he was really innocent, it was a question of whether the killer would get to him before I did him some real damage.

He pinched the bridge of his nose and sighed. "I'm young, free and single. I like to think of life as a buffet. I'll try a little of this and a little of that. I'm not going to eat smoked salmon for the rest of my life. Sometimes I want a burger."

"And that night, Lila was a burger?" Wiggles asked. I was pleased to see that he looked as unimpressed with Drayton as I felt.

"I guess so. We made out for a while, it was fun, then we heard the commotion and that was how we both saw that Greasy had died," Drayton said as he examined a bottle of Champagne, then added it to a suitcase.

"And Lila will vouch for that?"

"I've no idea. She might want to protect her reputation as Greasy's devastated lady in mourning. I'm sure other people saw, though. We weren't very discreet about it."

"But this morning, you're quite sure that you were alone and that nobody can confirm where you were?" I asked.

"Yes, unfortunately. Even I must spend a rare night alone."

"Can you see how this all looks? A man's found killed outside your business, you have no alibi and we come over and find you packing your things?"

"It looks to me like the actions of a sensible man. A spate of murders targeted on the food industry? I'd be mad to stick around."

"How's your knowledge of reindeers?" I asked.

"What? I have no knowledge of reindeers," Drayton said.

"You can't handle them?"

"No! I'm useless in that department. No experience at all.

Is that relevant? If you're looking for a reindeer handler, it's Lila you need to speak to."

"Twisty was trampled to death by a reindeer," Wiggles revealed.

Drayton took that in for a moment before giving a low whistle. "Well, trust me, if anyone's trained a reindeer well enough to do that on command, it's Lila."

"We do have to make you aware that you've been named by someone else we've spoken to. Your potential motive seems to be common knowledge, Drayton. You're a real suspect in this case," I explained.

Drayton gasped. "Seriously? Look, I'm a ladies man and a bit of a cad. I know that, I accept that. I just love women. But I haven't hurt anyone - other than breaking a few hearts, I've hurt nobody. I'm a lover, not a fighter."

"That's all we want to say for now, but you need to stick around. You're under investigation. Unpack those cases and return home."

"I can't! Don't you understand that my life is at risk?" He exclaimed.

"I can get you a police guard outside the house or offer you a bed in Candy Cane Custody. What would you prefer?" Wiggles offered.

"Take me to custody," Drayton said. He held out his hands to be handcuffed, but Wiggles shook his head.

We trailed out of Sleigh A While and all crammed ourselves into the Fiat, with Drayton's long legs almost reaching the steering wheel from the back seat.

"Do you have any other music?" Drayton asked.

Wiggles turned to him and scowled. "There are some questions I don't dignify with a response."

The rest of the drive was a silent one and when we reached Candy Cane Custody, Wiggles drove into the back entrance, where prison guards greeted us and opened the back door for Drayton.

"Thank you for this, I appreciate it," he said to us as he untangled himself and clambered out of the tiny car.

We waited until he'd been escorted into the building, then Wiggles looked at me and raised an eyebrow.

"He puts on a good show of a man being afraid," Wiggles said.

"My thoughts exactly," I agreed.

"He wasn't honest about everything, though."

"No?"

"Claiming not to have any experience with reindeer! This is Candy Cane Hollow. Our children have basic reindeer training mastered before they can walk sometimes."

"All children?" I asked.

"It's taught in school. Reindeer are such an essential part of life here."

"Why would he lie about that?"

"Desperate people tell lies. I always joke that my job would be a heck of a lot easier if people told me the truth."

I laughed. "I bet that would remove a lot of the fun, though."

"That's true! Now, Holly, I appreciate you waking up so early to help me out. Where can I take you?"

"I'll head home, I think," I said.

"Good choice," Wiggles said, and then he turned up the volume and we sang along with George Michael.

## 15

Back at Claus Cottage, the house was very quiet and I wondered if I might be the only person around.

I settled down on the settee in the den and picked up my phone. No messages and no missed calls.

I grabbed a piece of paper and a novelty Santa pen and tried to get my thoughts in order.

Greasy had been killed. It seemed that that much was now obvious.

I got no further than that before the front door burst open, bringing inside a hunky dimpled man and a cold blast of air.

"Hey, you're back!" Nick said as he stomped out of his boots and peeled off his snow-covered jacket.

"Hey, you," I said. I felt coy and a little embarrassed that he'd witnessed my early morning grumpiness. Not to mention my early morning bedhead of a hairdo.

"You're busy?" He tipped his head towards the notepad.

"I'm trying to get my thoughts organised, but it might help to talk them through if you have a few minutes?"

"There's always time," he said with a wink.

"Great!"

"Shall I get us a drink?"

"That would be amazing," I agreed. A hot mug to hold would warm up my frosty hands.

He disappeared into the kitchen and my phone rang.

"Hey, August!" I greeted.

"I've been sitting here by the phone for days..." she said.

"You've what? Why? What's happening?"

"You promised me all of the details after your New Year's Eve date with Mr Hunkalicious! Do I take it from your silence that things went incredibly well, you saucy minx? He doesn't have you chained to a bed, does he?"

I felt my cheeks flame and hoped that her voice hadn't carried through to the kitchen.

"No, no, nothing like that! And I don't think that's how I referred to him either," I said.

"Mr Hunkalicious? Maybe it's how you should refer to him. You've clearly got the hots for him."

"Oh, yes, I won't try and deny that," I chose my words carefully.

"Hold on, why are you being so weird? Wait! Oh-Em-Gee! He's there, isn't he? He's right there?"

"Well, he's not right here. He's just making us a drink."

"Making you a drink! Holly Wood, you clever little girl! Please share all of your man training secrets with me," August said with a laugh.

"It's so good to hear your voice," I said.

"Aww, big sis! I see that being in love has made you sentimental."

"I'm not in..."

"Um hmm, tell it to someone who will believe your no-good lies. I knew you were in love the first time you clapped eyes on Billy Branson and I've known ever since."

"I was twelve when Billy Branson moved in next door," I reminded her.

"And you were a sucker for dark brown eyes and a knack with a football, even back then."

I laughed. "You're rotten!"

"I'm just pleased for you. Now, can you tell me everything or do you need to find ten minutes to prise yourself away from his lips first?"

I shook my head and rolled my eyes, even though August could see neither gesture. "I'll call you later."

"You promise? Because I'm here in baby land with nothing to do other than organise teeny tiny socks into matching pairs. A little romance to hear about would be quite nice right now."

"I promise. I'll call you soon. And I love you."

"I love you too, big sis."

Nick returned to the room as I ended the call. He held two mugs of strong coffee and handed one across to me.

"Were you talking to yourself?" He asked with a grin.

"My sister. I'll give her a call back later."

"Are you sure? I can give you some space now if you want," he offered. I was constantly impressed by how welcome he had made me feel in his house.

"No, really. I want to run through this. Are you sure you have time?"

"I always have time for you," he said.

I swallowed and tried to stay focused. "I don't know how much you know, but the second death today? It's Twisty. He was killed right outside Sleigh A While. He was trampled by a reindeer."

"Goodness. That's awful."

I nodded. "Peggy-Sue found his body on her early

morning walk, and Wiggles wanted me to be around to interview her with him."

"That's amazing. He obviously shares my opinion of how incredible you are! How did it go?"

"Well, we ended up deciding that Drayton was the prime suspect and that it would make sense for him to try and escape. So we went across there..."

"Wait. You went to try and catch the killer? Holly, I'm so proud of you investigating but you need to be sensible. I don't want you to get hurt."

"I won't," I said, with a nonchalant bat of my hand. It hadn't entered my head that we could have been in danger going after Drayton.

"I mean it. I couldn't stand to lose you. I've only just found you and I don't want to let you go."

"Okay," I said, as my stomach flipped. How was I supposed to concentrate with Mr Hunkalicious saying things like that to me? And yes, I had to give August credit, Mr Hunkalicious was a fine name for a fine man.

"What happened? Did you find Drayton?"

I nodded. "He was packing suitcases and preparing to flee."

"So he did do it?"

"He says not. He says that the murders are clearly targeting people in the food industry and he fears that he'll be next. Wiggles offered him protection but Drayton chose to be taken into Candy Cane Custody for his own safety."

"Wow. I mean, voluntarily going to prison? That's like the ultimate bluff if he is the murderer," Nick said.

"It's so strange, isn't it. He's either a master bluffer, or he's telling the truth."

"Do you have any other suspects?" Nick asked.

"Well, I think the person who found the body is always worth considering. And then there's Lila."

"Lila?"

"She had motive and opportunity to kill Greasy. She was still upset about their break-up. And Twisty was trampled by a very well-trained reindeer."

"Lila does have a flair with the reindeer," Nick agreed.

"I've seen. I just can't work out what her motive to hurt Twisty could be."

"Hmm," Nick murmured. He took a long sip of his coffee but remained silent. If he'd hoped the caffeine would give him insights, it had let him down.

"Oh, listen to this. Drayton told us that at the moment the glitter ball came down, he was kissing Lila!"

Nick raised an eyebrow. "Wow. Well, they're both innocent if that's true, surely?"

"I guess. I wasn't sure whether I believed him. I believe he'd have kissed her if he had half the chance, but would Lila have given him that chance?"

"Why don't we go and ask her?" Nick suggested.

We finished the rest of our coffees and bundled ourselves back into outdoor clothes, then made the short sleigh ride across to The Reindeer Run.

A man watched us from the farmhouse window as Nick brought the sleigh to a gentle stop. He was at the door a moment later, dressed in a grey string vest and a pair of trousers caked in mud.

"Everything alright there, Santa?"

"Hey Gus, is Lila around?" Nick asked.

Gus shrugged his lean shoulders. "She's around, but I couldn't say where exactly. Want me to go and find her?"

"That's okay, you stay inside in the warm. Are you happy for us to look for her?"

"Sure thing. This kinda time, she might be in the Top Field, or she could still be rounding up the troops from the stables. They'd be my guesses," he said.

"That's helpful. Thank you."

Gus watched from the doorway as we carefully walked across towards the stables.

We heard Lila before we saw her. She was singing a Christmas carol in a beautiful voice, and as we got closer it was clear that she was singing to the reindeer.

Nick cleared his throat to alert her to our presence, and she turned and gave us a self-conscious look.

"You guys make a habit of sneaking up on people?"

"Sorry. You have a beautiful voice, you shouldn't be embarrassed," Nick complimented her.

"Well, thanks. These guys are the only ones who ever hear me sing. And Greasy did. Do you have any news?"

Nick glanced at me and it was clear he was going to leave the questioning to me.

I stood a little straighter. "There's been a development. Another death."

Her hand shot to her mouth and her eyes grew wide. If it wasn't genuine shock, it was a very good impression.

"Who is it? Who died?"

"It was Twisty," I said.

Her brow furrowed. "Why would anyone want to hurt Twisty?"

"Who said anyone did? I said another death, not a murder," I asked.

Her eyes flittered around the stable then settled back on to my face. "It has to be murder. Either that, or Twisty was so upset he took his own life. They couldn't both have died from natural causes just days apart."

I cocked my head. It was a fair assumption.

"What happened to him?" Lila asked again. Her voice had grown quiet and immature, almost childlike.

"He was trampled by a reindeer," I said.

"Oh, no," Lila said. Her legs gave way and she dropped to a bale of hay inside the stable. The reindeer beside her in the stall watched her curiously.

"Wiggles has asked me to help him investigate and I have a few questions for you," I explained. Lila made no response.

"Where were you between 5am and 6am today?" I asked.

"I was right here. I'm always here before then. Why are you asking me this?"

"It's routine questions so we can get a picture of who was where, who might have seen something..."

"...and who might have done it? Am I a suspect?"

"Should you be?" I asked.

She swallowed and shook her head. "I'd have no reason to hurt Twisty."

"Does that mean you did have a reason to hurt Greasy?"

"Sure," she admitted. "I had a reason, but I didn't act on it. He dumped me and I wanted him back."

"And that's motive for murder?" I asked.

She shrugged. "I've seen things on TV, people who snap. And part of me understands it. If I'd thought about Greasy moving on and falling in love with someone else, I can almost understand the urge to stop it all."

"If you can't have him, nobody can?" I said.

"Exactly. In a strange way, it's understandable. But I could never have hurt him. That man meant everything to me. Well, him and these animals."

"And you were definitely here this morning?"

"One hundred percent. Ask Gus. He was around too."

"You're kind of the first person who comes to mind when you think of well-trained reindeer," I said.

Lila wrinkled her nose. "My reindeer dance and perform. They're like athletes. I would never abuse an animal by turning it into a weapon. Whoever did this is no animal lover, I can tell you that."

"That's an interesting point. And how about when the glitter ball came down, do you remember where you were then?"

Lila opened her mouth, then closed it again and paused. "I was working that night, so I was racing around. I don't remember exactly where I was when I heard the commotion."

"We've had a report that you were near the toilets kissing Drayton," I said.

Lila's cheeks flamed. "Absolutely not. He is the direct opposite of everything I'd look for in a man."

"Nobody's suggesting you were planning to marry him," Nick said with a smile.

"I can't stand men like him."

"He's very charming," I said.

"Exactly. I hate it. No, I was nowhere near Drayton," Lila said.

"When I heard it, I did wonder why you would do such a thing. And then I wondered if it was a way of making Greasy jealous perhaps?"

Lila's shoulders slumped. "No. Our relationship was completely over in his head. He wouldn't have felt any jealousy."

"Were you drinking that night?" I asked.

"A little, I guess," Lila admitted.

"Is there any chance you kissed Drayton and don't remember?" Nick suggested.

"No way. Absolutely not a chance. I was nowhere near him," Lila insisted.

The reindeer moved across the stable and nudged at her face with its nose. She couldn't help but smile.

Whatever I suspected Lila could have done, it was obvious that she was animal mad.

"This guy needs to get out into the field. Are we done here?" Lila asked.

"I do have a couple more questions. Since you're such a reindeer expert, I thought you might be able to help with giving us ideas of who else would have the skill to get a reindeer to trample a person."

Lila considered the question as she idly stroked the reindeer. "It's probably not as hard as you might imagine. All you'd need is... let me show you. Follow me."

Lila opened the stable door and clicked for the reindeer to follow her. In the open space of the stable yard, she demonstrated how to get the reindeer to stay fixed in one place and then repeatedly stand on its back legs and crash his front legs back to the ground.

"Now imagine that, but with a person under those front legs," Lila said.

"And that's not a high level of reindeer training?" I asked.

"Intermediate, maybe? There would be dozens of people in town who could do that. Everyone in Candy Cane Hollow has reindeer experience, remember."

"Well, that makes things harder than I thought."

"Were you thinking I was the only person who could make a reindeer do that?" Lila asked with a smile.

"Maybe," I admitted.

"There are definitely things that only I can get a reindeer to do, but those moves aren't it."

"Does it bother you that people have given your name?

That you've been implicated in a murder investigation?" I asked.

"Of course it does. A while ago, right after Greasy ended our relationship, I'd have confessed to anything and been happy to be locked away. But I've realised that losing him is enough loss. I want to be alive and free."

"If you're not the killer, Lila, who do you think did it?"

"It's Drayton. He wants The Greasy Spoon closed down. Who else would benefit from both Greasy and Twisty being dead?" Lila answered without so much as a pause.

"You've been very helpful," I said.

"I really have to get into the field now," she said. The reindeer by her side was perfectly trained but like a coiled spring. It was obvious that the beast needed to run.

"That's fine. Thanks for speaking to us."

Lila made one tiny hand gesture and the reindeer sprinted away towards the field.

I shook my head as we watched Lila walk after it. "She really is something."

"What do you think?" Nick asked.

"I think she just gave us the key to this whole case," I said with a nod of my head.

"Really?"

Gus was on the doorstep again as we returned to the sleigh. "All okay, Santa?"

"All okay," Nick called.

"Oh, Gus, what time did Lila start work today?"

Gus looked up at the sky, as if a cloud might have the answer. "Couldn't tell you. Early. Why?"

"She mentioned being here before 5am. That's really early to start work," I said.

"Not in farming, it's not. If she said she was here, she was here."

"But you didn't see her?"

"You know what I was doing at five this morning? Mending a fence over on the East side. This place is sprawling and every inch of it needs checking every day. So, no, I wasn't here with a cup of tea to greet her, but if she said she was here, she was here. Alright?"

"Alright," I said. I felt as if I'd very much been told off, but his loyalty towards his member of staff was touching. I just hoped it wasn't misplaced.

"We'll leave you to it," Nick said. He offered me his hand to help me climb up into the sleigh, and we were on our way within moments.

"I couldn't be a farmer. All those long hours outside in the cold, it must be tough," I said as Nick guided the sleigh down the snowy streets.

"It's hard work, that's for sure. Where shall we go now?"

"Do you want to come with me to speak to another person? I think I know who did it."

"I think you should hand it over to Wiggles," Nick said.

"I'm not in danger," I said.

"You're talking about confronting a murderer. You've got no idea how much danger you could be in. Look, Holly, I love that you're doing this and you're obviously good at it, but you do have to be sensible."

"I am being sensible. I'm going to go and speak to this person with a big, strapping man by my side," I squeezed his arm as I spoke.

"Oh, jingle bells. Are you trying to flatter me into agreeing with you?"

I gave him a wink. "Maybe."

"Fine, I'll go with you on two conditions. We call Wiggles so he knows where we're going, and you tell me how you know who did it."

"I can agree to those terms. Lila said that nobody who loved animals would use a reindeer as a murder weapon. Something like that, anyway."

"I remember," Nick said.

"And that's how I know who did it," I said.

Nick looked at me with confusion, but I told him where to head to, and he followed my instructions as I rang Wiggles to alert him.

## 16

Nick parked the sleigh up the street, out of sight of the place we were about to go to.

"What's the plan? Shall we wait for Wiggles?" He asked.

"No, let's go in now. Just let me lead. I can do this," I said, my voice firm and confident.

"I know you can," Nick said. He leaned across the sleigh and kissed me, and I closed my eyes and saw stars. There was really nothing I wanted more than to remain in that sleigh kissing him for hours, but I had to catch the killer.

I pulled myself away from Mr Hunkalicious and climbed down from the sleigh.

We were on a quiet street right on the border of the Festive Forest, and other than a couple of net curtains twitching as we walked by, the street was deserted.

The house we approached had an immaculate air about it. A clear path had been cut through the snow from the gate to the front door, and even the outside windowsills were snow-free.

A camera on the top of the house shifted position as it

spotted movement, and a red light flashed on and off as it focused its gaze on us.

"We're being watched," I whispered. Nick followed my gaze.

In that fraction of a moment, as our attention was elsewhere, a crash rang out from behind the house.

"Suspect is on the move!" I shouted, and I raced down the front path and hammered on the door. I tried the handle but it was locked.

"We have to get to the back," Nick exclaimed.

An old man appeared at the house next door and watched us.

"Can you help us, sir? We need access to the back," Nick asked.

The old man leaned on a whisper of a walking stick and considered us as if we may be burglars.

"Nick Claus, is that you?"

"We don't have time for this," I muttered. I trailed back down the path and across to the old man's house. Nick followed.

"It's me, sir. Can we just walk through your house to get to the back garden?" Nick asked.

"Anything for a Claus," the old man said. He stood aside and let us enter.

I thundered down his tiny hall and into the galley kitchen. The back door key was in the door, and the door wasn't even locked.

I pushed the door open and looked at the Festive Forest. A real life forest where every single tree was decorated, year-round, with baubles and tinsel. It was quite the sight.

"There!" I said as I saw movement not far ahead of us.

"Let's go," Nick said.

We moved as quickly as we could, but nobody had

cleared a path through the forest and the snow was up past our knees. Our progress was frustratingly slow, but luckily it was just as slow for the figure moving ahead in a desperate bid to get away.

"Stop! We need to speak to you! Stay where you are!" I called.

"We can't do this much longer, Holly. Frostbite and exposure don't care whether you're on official police business or not, they'll still get you."

I sighed with frustration. "But we're so close!"

Nick pursed his lips. "Five more minutes."

"Can you try shouting?" I asked.

He cleared his throat. Already our voices were growing weak from the cold. I couldn't feel my feet.

"This is Nick Claus. You're being asked to come back down right away. This is an official Claus request," he said.

"Is that a thing? An official Claus request?" I asked.

He nodded. "We try not to use them. But they come in handy occasionally. It holds the same weight as a police order."

I watched as the shape up ahead stopped, turned, and then raised a hand and waved at us, before starting to stomp through the snow back towards us.

"It worked," I gasped.

Nick shrugged with modesty.

"Nicholas! Were you calling for me?" Peggy-Sue asked as she reached us. She was shivering uncontrollably and I realised that we all had to get our legs out of the snow right away.

We made our way back down to Peggy-Sue's house and crowded around her log fire. The house was as immaculate inside as outside.

"Why were you running?" I asked.

"Running? I was just having a stroll. I like to check on the baubles," Peggy-Sue said.

"You were running. Tell us why," Nick said.

"I saw something. I was scared that the killer was coming for me."

"And why would they do that?" I asked.

"Because I found Twisty. Maybe the killer thinks I could have seen something. I was in fear for my life and I made a run for it. I'd never have ran away from a Claus."

"We're here to ask you some questions," I said.

"I've already told Wiggles everything I know," Peggy-Sue said.

"You've told him one version, but I'm here for the truth."

"I don't know what you mean," she said.

"You told me you have no experience with reindeer," I reminded her.

"I don't. I have a phobia."

"A phobia?"

"That's right. Terrified of the filthy things, I am. I couldn't go near one," Peggy-Sue said.

"That's interesting. Because you told me and Wiggles that you were allergic."

"I am! That too!" Peggy-Sue said with a nervous laugh.

"Allergic and phobic? That's unlucky," Nick said.

"Yes, I guess so. What does that have to do with anything?"

"Everyone in Candy Cane Hollow has reindeer experience. You thought you could lie to me about that because I'm new here."

Peggy-Sue blinked at me but said nothing.

"The truth is, you don't like reindeers. You probably don't like any animals because they get dirty and they smell

and they shed hair. But you have enough reindeer knowledge to have caused poor Twisty's death," I said.

I saw a flash of movement outside the window as
Wiggles slowly passed by in his Fiat.

"And why would I have wanted to hurt Twisty?" Peggy-
Sue said.

I nodded slowly. "That's been the question, hasn't it? You
had the motive to kill Greasy, but I can't find any reason
you'd want Twisty dead. And then I realised, that's why you
did it. You killed Twisty to cast suspicion elsewhere, and
over to Drayton specifically."

"I don't know what you're talking about," Peggy-Sue said.

"You wanted Greasy dead because you couldn't stand
someone complaining about you. His letter to the Chronicles made you furious. How dare he complain about you!
Complaining is your job, your civic duty. You wanted him
dead but you thought the glitter ball crash would look like
an accident."

"This is an interesting story but it has nothing to do with
me. And I will complain. I'll be filing a report with Wiggles
about the use of civilians to do police work."

"It was a clever idea, I'll give you that. You were up there
on the beams but as soon as that glitter ball fell, everyone's
attention was focused on Greasy. You slipped down the
stairs without anyone noticing," Nick said.

"Exactly. And you nearly got away with it being considered an accident. But when I started to investigate whether it
could have been foul play, that's when you panicked. You
were scared that I'd work it out. Twisty's death was the ultimate red herring."

"And on what evidence are you here suggesting I'm the
murderer when it's quite clearly Drayton?" Peggy-Sue asked.

"Drayton was so scared that he could have been the

third victim, he voluntarily took himself off to Candy Cane Custody," I explained.

Peggy-Sue clicked her tongue. "What a wimp."

"Yes, what a wimp indeed. But he'd have had no reason to be so scared if he was the killer."

"He's a good actor, then. Maybe that's why so many ladies fall for his charms. Serial killers are often charismatic, you know."

"Know a lot about serial killers, do you?" Nick asked.

"What? No! I just heard that on the radio once. You can't seriously think that I'm a cold-blooded killer."

"I think in your head, you're not a killer. It's interesting that you didn't actually touch either of them. You used other things as your weapons. But, then, you're so hygiene focused, of course you'd do that."

Peggy-Sue looked beyond me and out of the window as Wiggles drove by again. It seemed that he was either struggling to find the address, or having issues finding a parking space - which was hard to believe given he was driving a car about the size of a matchbox.

"I simply want what's best for Candy Cane Hollow. You may mock me for insisting that things are just right, but I do it so that others strive for higher standards," Peggy-Sue said.

"What was it about Greasy's letter that annoyed you so much?" I asked.

"It was the style not the substance. I accept his point. My complaints do have an impact on local businesses, as they should. If Bruce wants to sell more baubles, he shouldn't engage in false advertising. My reports keep the standards high. But I don't think that Greasy had even checked his letter for spelling errors!"

"That's what annoyed you?" I asked in disbelief.

"Of course it is. The grammar was awful. He had double

negatives in there and his sentence structure was childish. I have had letters rejected by the Chronicles before, can you believe that? They have rejected me and accepted him and his amateur wittering. It was an absolute mockery of true journalism."

"Peggy-Sue, you told me you hadn't seen the letter," I reminded her.

Her eyes flicked to a box on the coffee table, then she gasped. "I bought a back copy. I told you I would."

"Back copies take two weeks to be delivered," Nick said.

I frowned at him.

"My mum keeps a folder of all of the editions that mention me, and she's missed a few before. Had to order the back copies. There's this whole archive process. Anyway..."

"What's in the box?" I asked.

Peggy-Sue kept her eyes fixed on me and tried to look nonchalant. "Nothing."

I reached down and picked it up. The box was stuffed full of paper clippings. It was a memory box containing all of Peggy-Sue's complaint letters, and right there at the top was Greasy's letter.

"You did this?" I held up the clipping for Peggy-Sue to see.

She nodded. She had edited Greasy's letter in red pen, picking out spelling errors and what she had called *lazy and predictable word choices*.

There was a sticky note on the clipping and in writing that was much clunkier than her own, someone had responded to her suggested edits:

*Ya can take these and stick them up you're Candy Cane hollow!!!!!!!!!!!!!!*

"Do you see what I was dealing with?" Peggy-Sue asked.

"You found the response offensive?"

"I certainly did. He used the wrong 'your' and didn't capitalise Hollow. Not to mention the attack on my decency that all of those exclamation marks present."

"Greasy wrote this note?" I asked.

"No comment," Peggy-Sue said.

"We can get a handwriting sample done easily enough. If that's Greasy's handwriting, there's no point denying it."

"Fine, it's his. The little toe rag couldn't resist the chance to show his stupidity again!"

"So you had seen the letter before he died," I said.

"Huh?"

"You've seen the letter, edited it and sent it to him, and he's responded. All of that happened before he was killed," I broke it down for her.

"It's no loss to anyone! He was a cantankerous elf and not much use to anyone. The Greasy Spoon would have been better off without him. That old girlfriend of his, she could do so much better, even if she does have an unnatural obsession for reindeer. I didn't see the harm."

"You didn't see the harm in killing him?" I pushed.

She shrugged.

"And how about Twisty? I'm right that he just got caught up in your attempts to avoid suspicion?"

"Now, I do feel bad about Twisty. I had nothing against him at all. But self-preservation is hard wired into us. I had little choice," Peggy-Sue said.

"How did you get him to meet you?" Nick asked.

"I do always go out walking at that time, so I knew the streets would be empty. I told him I had news about Greasy's death. He was so easy to fool he probably deserved what came."

"And the reindeer?"

"Just a neighbour's. She knew nothing about it. I'd borrowed him and returned him before she woke up."

"We're going to have to take you to Candy Cane Custody. You know that, right?"

"Do you think it was too obvious doing it right outside Sleigh A While? I did wonder about that. But I wanted to point towards Drayton, because goodness gumdrops we need to get rid of him."

I glanced at Nick.

"Get rid of him? Why?"

"He's leaving a trail of broken hearts around Candy Cane Hollow! He takes a lady's number and then doesn't call her. He has no respect for women," Peggy-Sue said.

"Has he done something to you?" I asked.

Peggy-Sue glared at me as if the question was stupid. "He'd never have a chance with me. I'd eat a man like him for breakfast."

"I'm sure you would," I agreed.

She sighed. "My daughter works for him. He's been... inappropriate. He was the obvious person to have killed them both, and if you had just followed the clues and charged him, we'd be rid of him too!"

"Would your daughter speak to the police?" Nick asked.

"Absolutely not. Summer doesn't want any repercussions. Which is why I was sorting it all out for her."

"Well, Drayton's in custody. We have some time to look into that. But let's get back to what you've done. You've killed two men."

Peggy-Sue flared her nostrils and glanced past me again. I followed her gaze and saw that Wiggles had parked up opposite the house and was unfolding himself from the Fiat.

"No!" Nick cried.

I spun around and saw that Peggy-Sue had made a run

for it. I watched as she ran into the tiny kitchen and tried to open the door.

Luckily, I'd pocketed the key when we'd brought her back inside.

I watched in horror as she backed up and then threw herself into the full glass panel with all of her strength. The glass shattered and she fell through it, into the garden.

Nick and I were after her, but she had a lead and we watched as she darted back into the Festive Forest.

Wiggles was behind us, having let himself in the unlocked front door. "That her?"

"That's her. Shall we follow?" I panted.

"No. You've already been in there once. I'm not letting you risk it again. Wiggles and I will go," Nick said.

"I came prepared," Wiggles said. He had protective trousers on and he passed a pair to Nick, who slipped them on over the clothes he already wore.

"I can help," I said.

"Stay here, Holly. That's an official Claus request," Nick said. He leaned in and kissed me and then he was gone.

Wiggles was far more sprightly than I'd have expected, given his fairly rotund shape, and they dashed through the snow and into the forest.

I watched until I couldn't see them any longer, and I carried on watching until the sky grew navy and then black.

Eventually, I closed the door and returned to the fire, feeling guilty for enjoying warmth while they were out battling the elements.

I decided to busy myself by looking through Peggy-Sue's memory box. I read letters of complaint about the official town colours not being festive enough one year, about the residents on her street not clearing snow from their drives, and about the carol singers being too loud and out of tune.

There was a noise out back and I jumped to my feet.

In the garden, Nick and Wiggles carried Peggy-Sue. Nick's eyebrows had icicles attached to them and Wiggles' cheeks were the reddest things I'd ever seen.

"Call an ambulance," Nick grunted to me.

I grabbed my phone and dialled right away as they carried Peggy-Sue in and laid her some distance from the fire.

"Shouldn't she be closer to the heat?" I asked.

"She has to get warm gradually. This is the most dangerous bit," Nick explained.

He stood by the fire and Wiggles joined him.

Peggy-Sue's skin was blue and her eyes were closed. The tips of her fingers had begun to blacken.

"Are you two okay?" I asked, my voice barely audible. I was terrified.

"We'll be fine," Nick said.

"Hazard of the job," Wiggles added.

I gave the operator the address and we did the only thing we could.

We waited for help to arrive.

## 17

I sat in Wiggles' office and told him what I'd witnessed.

"These are serious allegations," Wiggles said as he wrote my statement out by hand.

"I know," I said. I had decided to go on the record to report Drayton's behaviour. I owed it to Summer.

"I'll have a word with Drayton and see what he has to say. In fact, I'll do it now before I finish for the day."

"Sounds like you have some plans?"

"It's the Figure Skating competition tonight. I need to spend some time getting myself mentally composed. I have a pre-competition routine that involves a hot bubble bath and a little..."

"Let me guess. Last Christmas?"

"How did you know?" Wiggles asked.

"Just an instinct I had," I laughed.

"Will you come? There's always room for the Claus family in the VIP section."

"I'd love to," I said. I wasn't part of the Claus family, and Wiggles knew it, but I didn't want to correct him.

"Right. Wait here. I'll be back," Wiggles said and he set off out of the room to question Drayton.

I sat alone in Wiggles' bare office then pulled my phone out of my pocket.

I was going to message Nick and ask if he could join me at the Figure Skating competition, but I realised there was something else I needed to do first.

I dialled the number and listened as the line rang and rang and rang.

*You're through to August. I can't speak right now but if you leave your name and number after the tone, I'll get back to you within 72 hours.*

I laughed. "Hey sis. You're the only person I know who gives a timeframe on their personal voicemail! I was just calling to tell you all about Mr Hunkalicious. I guess I'll hear from you within 72 hours! Love you, bye!"

The phone rang straight away and I answered with a laugh. "Desperate to hear about Mr Hunkalicious, huh?"

"Mr who?" Nick's voice filled my ear.

"Oh! It's you! I thought you were my sister," I said as my cheeks flamed.

"Who's this Mr Hunkaliffer?" Nick asked. I had no idea whether he'd genuinely misheard me or was saving my modesty but I was happy to play along.

"Oh, he's just someone I, erm, read about. Anyway, how are things?"

Nick had escorted Peggy-Sue and the paramedics to the hospital so that Wiggles could get back to Candy Cane Custody and make a good start on filing the paperwork.

"She's conscious. She woke up a few minutes ago," Nick said.

I felt myself exhale with relief. Sure, Peggy-Sue was a killer. But I wanted her in prison, not dead.

"Has she said anything?" I asked.

"She was very emotional. Cried and apologised. I think she realised that Summer's going to find out what she did."

"It's going to hit her hard. You don't think Peggy-Sue will try to change her story, say it wasn't her?"

"I don't think so. How are things going over there?"

"Well, Wiggles has invited me to watch the Figure Skating competition tonight and I can take a date with me," I teased.

"You can? Any idea who you might ask?"

"Ooh, I've been considering the options!" I laughed. "And there's really only one I'd consider. What do you say? Will you come?"

"You know I will," Nick said.

A stern voice piped up in the background and he gave a nervous laugh.

"Everything okay?" I asked.

"I've just been told off for being on my phone inside the hospital. I'll finish up here and see you back home?"

"Sure!" I said. I ended the call and suddenly felt a presence in the room with me.

Wiggles was in the doorway, a grin plastered on his face.

"What?" I asked.

"I'm just delighted you're coming tonight. Oh, and I'm also happy that Drayton's just given a full confession."

"You're kidding?"

Wiggles shook his head. "He's really fallen apart since Twisty's death. The man's a nervous wreck. I went in and mentioned Summer's name and he spilled every single thing, then went on to mention a fair few other ladies who he's treated terribly."

"What will happen?"

"He'll do a year or two in Custody and I've suggested he

might want to relocate in the future. He won't be troubling Candy Cane Hollow any more, put it that way."

"That's incredible," I said.

"We're making a pretty good team, hey?" Wiggles said.

I laughed. "We have done, but that'll have to stop now."

He looked at me with disappointment.

"The surgery opens next week. I'll be busy seeing patients again, not solving crimes."

"Ah, of course. Well hopefully there won't be any more crimes. Apart from the serious crime that is me wearing latex, of course!"

HE WASN'T LYING.

As soon as he took to the ice, it was clear that I would never get the image of Wiggles in latex out of my head. It was burned in to my brain.

But he had some moves.

He was a blur of glitter and gems as he spun and raced his way around the ice to the astonished applause from the audience.

It was clear he'd won before he was even halfway through his routine.

We joined the rest of the crowd and got to our feet and clapped in rhythm as he skated and whirled, jumped and twirled to the beat of his unsurprising music of choice.

By the time he finished his set and did a lap of the rink bowing at the spectators, my hands ached from all of the clapping I'd done.

Wiggles reached the VIP section, where Nick and I had been given front row seats, and did a bow. The top of his head glistened under the lights and beads of sweat twinkled.

"You were amazing!" I called out, but he couldn't hear me over the crowd.

We returned to our seats and watched the other contestants, all of whom were excellent and yet not as good as Wiggles. We clapped and cheered and enjoyed their skill, and at some point Nick reached across and took my hand in his.

I looked at him and smiled, then had an idea.

I pulled out my phone and leaned in to Nick so my head was next to his.

"Smile!" I commanded as I took the selfie.

We examined the image afterwards and I felt my heart skip a beat. We looked right together, as if everything that had happened to us had laid a path so we would find each other.

"Bathroom break," Nick whispered and left his seat.

With him out of sight, I sent the photo to August. Just the image of me and the man who I was quickly believing was The One. I included no message, no explanation.

I figured that sometimes, no words were needed.

THE END
Order the next book in the series now!

## DEAR CHRONICLE READERS

Your probably wandering why I didn't not write this letter sooner.

Let's just say there's some KETCHING UP to do!

I've had enough of Peggy-Sue! This woman is hurting my business and you'res too.

She complains about everything and nothing and everything in between.

One time, I knew it was her in my Unnamed Business, and I added a hair from my own head inside her sammich! She didn't even no it was there!

I think that proves that her complaints are false and malishus.

What can we do about this woman?

I'll consider all options to keep our businesses open! Except the Slay A While because they charge too much for frothy coffee with a fancy name.

You'res,

Anonymus

# CHRISTMAS MYSTERY BONUSES

Help yourself to a festive fun pack, available exclusively at:

https://dl.bookfunnel.com/9ckxf7kcfh

Ho-ho-hope you enjoy it!

Mona x

# ABOUT THE AUTHOR

Mona Marple is a lover of all things book-related. When she isn't working on her next release, she's probably curled up somewhere warm reading a good story.

Mona is a fan of all things festive and is looking forward to adding to the Christmas Cozy Mystery series over the years. Her other cozy mysteries include the Waterfell Tweed series, the Mystic Springs paranormal series, the co-written A Witch In Time paranormal series, and the Mexican Mysteries series.

Mona lives in Nottinghamshire, England with her bread baking husband, her always-singing daughter, and their pampered Labradoodle, Coco. In fact, Mona's online reader group were a big part of persuading Mona's husband to welcome Coco into their home!

facebook.com/monamarpleauthor

instagram.com/monamarple